Jesse Jameson

and the
Vampire Vault

Sean Wright

A Crowswing Book

LET THE JOURNEY BEGIN ...

By Sean Wright and available from Crowswing Books

Jesse Jameson Series

Otherwise known as the

Jesse Jameson

Alpha to Omega Series

(Reading order)

Jesse Jameson and the Golden Glow

Jesse Jameson and the Bogie Beast

Jesse Jameson and the Curse of Caldazar

Jesse Jameson and the Vampire Vault

Jesse Jameson and the Stonehenge of Spelfindial

Jesse Jameson and the Earthwitch of Evenstorm

Jesse Jameson and the Walkers of the Worlds

Other fiction:

The Twisted Root of Jaarfindor (2004)

Dark Tales of Time and Space (2005)

This book is dedicated to Helen, Vince,
Adam, Jason, Rhys and Owen.

First published in paperback in 2004 by
Crowswing Books.

10 9 8 7 6 5 4 3 2 1

www.crowswingbooks.co.uk

First Edition

Text Copyright © Sean Wright 2004

Illustrations Copyright © Sean Wright 2004

The moral rights of the author and illustrator have been asserted.

A CIP catalogue record for this book is available
from the British Library.

ISBN 0-9544374-7-0

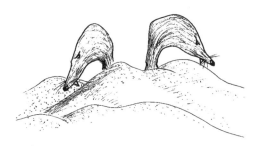

There be vampires lurking in the shadows,

dark things crawling from the ground

Praise for Sean Wright

'Part of the new wave of children's authors ... highly collectable.' *Book and Magazine Collectors*

'As always, I love the black and white sketches of magical and monstrous creatures scattered through the book. Packed with hyperactive action and horrific monsters...' *Hilary Williamson, bookloons.com*

'Jesse Jameson's journey ... is eventful and in places downright hair-raising.' *Curled Up With A Good Book*

'Highly recommended,' *GP Taylor, bestselling author of Shadowmancer.*

One

Wildhunt

The Skaardrithadon glided deeper and deeper into stifling cloud, and Jesse flew after him. All she could think about was Perigold, now a vampire slave. The thought made her feel sick. In her hands, Jesse Jameson held the black obsidian pyramid. Each time she closed the gap between them, its point flashed blood red. Once it had lit up a luminous green and stopped flashing. She had been within a few hundred yards of him, but somehow in the foggy mirk he'd escaped again. Still she flew on as her dragon self.

Jesse glanced over her spiny shoulder and looked at her companions. It had been a long and difficult journey in the gloomy mists of the Skaardrithadon's ever expanding aura. But they had not faltered. Trondian-Yor and Iggywig were flying together beside a winged beast the wizard had fashioned from the ether of his magical mind. It was big and powerful, black and scaly, a cross between an eagle, a dragon, a horse and a tortoise. Its shell was speckled and enormous. Giant eagle wings flapped slowly and its

9

six horse's legs galloped for added speed.

Iggywig called the power of the creature's legs his 'turbo boostings.' Its noble head was that of a dragon, able to breathe fire and brimstone. Trondian-Yor had named his creature creation Cyren, because it wailed like a fire engine at approaching danger.

Behind them, sitting astride Cyren's tortoise shell back, the Dragon Hunter cradled Jake in his arms. Jake had not regained consciousness since he'd blacked out in the Innermost Sanctum back at Caldazar. Kumo Diaz sat astride the creature's neck, holding reins and looking as if he was steering, but both he and the others knew who was boss: Cyren had a mind of his own.

Jesse had no idea where they were now. They could have travelled for hours or days. There was no way of telling except Jesse was starving hungry and thirsty. Her mouth was as dry as an oven and it was painful to lick her lips because her tongue was tender and swollen.

'We should rest awhile,' Trondian-Yor said, breaking the silence.

'No,' Jesse said, her gaze locked on the luminous wafer-thin trail. 'We are getting closer.'

'True,' Kumo Diaz said. 'But Trondian-Yor speaks sense. We stop now for a while.'

Jesse ignored them, increasing her pace; wings flapping like great rhythmic heart beats. At the front of her thoughts was her grandfather, Perigold. She had to release him from his vampire state. Time was running out. Perhaps, it had already run out for all she knew. With no landscape or day or night, it was impossible to calculate time. Jake's wristwatch had stopped. It had frozen on 11:11 the second they'd entered the cloud. Like Jake, it was motionless.

'Jesse, did you hear Kumo?' Trondian-Yor said.

'Yes,' she said reluctantly. 'Eat as you fly. Drink, too. We can't stop. Perigold needs us.'

'But I'm sick of magical food,' Kumo Diaz said. 'It's great when you first eat it, but ten minutes later you're hungry again. It has no substance.'

Jesse ignored him, ignored Iggywig's reasons for stopping.

'But I be a-needing a call of naturings,' he said. 'Iggywig be a-needing a pee-pee.'

'Pee as you fly,' Jesse said, hiding a tiny grin. She raced on, focusing on the trail ahead.

Deep inside her, Jesse's hearts burned like a forest fire. It was a fire of rage and anger, she knew, and it was also a fire of aching pain and suffering. The anger came from her guilt. She had been too late to save Perigold from the Skaardrithadon. All she had needed to do was repeat the curse with Jake, but she'd failed. Her pain came from her guilt, too, the guilt of her powerlessness. She was just a child after all, as her companions had reminded her. What could she do against the might and magic of adult witches, warlocks, vampires and the like? She had in reality done plenty to stand up to the dark forces. But to her it felt a if she'd not done enough.

Her mind did not linger long on the Driths or the Bogie Beast. But she couldn't stop thinking about her grandfather. Her guilt was burning deep inside like a furnace filled with white hot molten steel. She wouldn't give up. She wouldn't let Perigold down this time. She wouldn't stop until she had replaced his vampire blood with fairy blood again. She had no idea how she was going to get the blood or perform the transfusion, but that mattered little at that moment in time. As Roger Jameson frequently said, she would cross that bridge when she came to it.

11

There were more pressing concerns. She had to find him first, and quickly. Later, she would decide what to do with the Skaardrithadon, the Curse of Caldazar, and the Obsidian Pyramid. But not now. Now she focused again on the luminous trail that corkscrewed like an antelope's horn within the cloud of darkness. Now she hurtled into the shadows alight with burning guilt.

*

From his lair, far from the trap he had set and the dark forces he'd commanded to follow Jesse Jameson, the Skaardrithadon was consumed with frantic impulses. He moulded the red and black marbled mist in his hands like clay. He worked fast. He shaped and twisted. He wiped his sweating brow with the back of his pallid hand. He smoothed the forming creature, with palms that sanded and planed like a carpenter. He pinched and plucked at the mist until the creature he had fashioned lay still and silent on the damp red earth.

It looked like an eight foot tall gargoyle, something seen glaring down from a church wall. Its grotesque features floated in and out of focus. The Skaardrithadon's work was not yet complete. He knelt down and stared hard at his misty creation, brooding with a growing storm in his eyes. He held his hands up over the creature's shifting body. He let a low groaning note rise up deep from the back of his throat. It sounded like pebbles beneath an ocean's breaking waves as they were dragged over and over the beach. His eyelids flickered, the whites rolling in their sockets. His lips were narrow and drawn and black. He coughed. He spluttered. He breathed a silver mist into the morphing creature. This life force transformed, became solid. But the solidity slackened. Like melt water it dribbled life into the creature's forming heart. His dark magic was working.

'A part of my glow I give to thee, vile creature.'

The dribble became a trickle, feeding a little more life into the creature. He waved symbols and signs in the thick warm air above it. Incantations tumbled with archaic ease, phrases so ancient that their guttural tones sounded like four-letter swear words.

'My soul I impart to thee.'

Evil, a thread of swirling darkness, left the Skaardrithadon. It crashed into the stirring creature's heart. It bucked, convulsed, spluttered.

'Come now to life! Do my bidding! Serve me!'

A huge crack like thunder rippled the earth beneath the creature. Spumes of red dust puffed up. Tiny flames ignited, sparked, licked life into its lifeless parts. It juddered, coughed, spluttered. Its narrow black eyes opened with a snap. In less time than a blinking eye it became flesh and bone, morphing out of the misty mould. Its yellow skin barely covered muscle, barely covered the work of arteries and veins beneath. But it was flesh and blood, of sorts, now. It was life. The creature howled like a demon and sat up, staring menacingly at its master. No, it stared *through* the Skaardrithadon, devoid of emotion. If looks could kill, the New Master of Darkness would have been dead instantly. But this creature did not possess such mind power. This creature was a hunter whose physical strength was greater than twenty men. It had been created to run, to hunt, to capture and kill.

'Yes – that's it.' The Skaardrithadon's voice was thick with a dark brooding tone. 'Come into this world. You are mine, creature from my glow. You will do my bidding and no-one else's. Do you understand?'

13

The creature howled its affirmation, exposing sharp black fangs. Its mouth was oozing blood and white froth, foaming as if it was overflowing with rabies. It beat its chest like a gorilla, growled and waited impatiently. Grunts, deep, wild.

'Find and hunt down the fairy child Jesse Jameson and her companions. Bring me the children – kill the rest. Feast on their blood!'

The Skaardrithadon paused a moment, a small flash of fear – a hesitation. Then he reached out and slapped his hand on the creature's bulbous head. He gripped it, and from his mind he transferred pictures and memories and thoughts and feelings. All were dark, all were clear. The creature had been given everything it needed to fulfil the hunt ahead. It saw Jesse Jameson plainly in its mind's eye.

'Go now! Bring me the children!'

The mottled creature roared. The New Master of Darkness curled his hand into a tight fist. He punched its chest and the creature laughed madly. It puffed out its chest even more, offering the Skaardrithadon a second chance to strike it without defence. He punched the creature as hard as he could, trying to knock it down. The creature didn't flinch, or rock, or sway. It was solid, as if he had thumped rock. It howled not in pain but in a mocking way, which if it had been capable of speech it would have said, 'Is that the best you can do, Master?' The Skaardrithadon sent a telepathic message to the creature which waited for a third blow. The third blow did not come. Turning, it spat blood and spittle to the earth like a dart and lumbered out of the lair into the storm-riddled twilight.

Dark purple and brown clouds foamed above the creature. It screamed in defiance at the forked

14

lightning and snarled and raised a mighty fist at the thunder claps. It feared neither the elements of nature nor the vampire creatures of the night. It feared neither magic nor mind control. It was absolutely fearless.

The Skaardrithadon did not watch the creature leave. Instead, he extracted more mist from himself, groaning, brooding. He moulded dozens of creatures from it. He performed the same ritual over and over. He brought them to life with portions of his glow and set them on their way to join the Wild Hunt. He created hundreds of creatures. He called them his Brood. He was close to complete exhaustion. But his work was done.

Something shifted in the shadows.

'Stay still,' the Skaardrithadon growled. 'Do not fight the change.'

Perigold's head appeared from the darkness of the depths of the lair. Long thin fangs were exposed from his open mouth. His eyes rolled in pain. His blood felt as if fire was burning its way along his arteries. Torrents of sweat glistened his pale ghost-like forehead. The vampire blood was strong, so much stronger than fairy blood. He felt as if he was losing his battle. He reached up a white claw of a hand and dug his nails into his cheek. He tugged at his flesh. The pain inside his body was excruciating. He screamed out Jesse's name in the darkness. It echoed horribly through the Skaardrithadon's lair.

Two

The Naargapire

Jesse clung to the aftermath of the Skaardrithadon's viscous trail. Like a snail gleam, instead of shining silver, it shone mucus green in the overcast fog. Only her dragon eyes could see the trail, and she felt grateful for her shape-shifting skills. Ever since entering the Kingdoms she'd been amazed and dazed by her ability, but never reflective. It was hard to be objective about the magical events and people she'd encountered. So many of the people in the fairy kingdoms were extra-ordinary. So many of them possessed extra-ordinary talents and gifts. To them, these talents were as natural as breathing. But to her, everything she saw was coloured with awe and wonder. And her magical talents were the most astounding of all. Perigold had claimed she would need training and he was right. In the shape-shifting challenge she'd proved a worthy student as she'd battled with Jagdrith and Bragga Huggaton. But now she wasn't certain how long she could hold her shape. She had been following her prey for hours. But for how many she

16

wasn't sure. Time was difficult to gauge in the smog-filled darkness. The strain of constantly following a vaporous trail was making her tired. Every now and again she felt her shape change beyond her control, realign, melt somewhat. She was sure her feet had dissolved to nothing more than blobs, but she didn't have the strength to look – in case her worst fears were true.

Still, Trondian-Yor and the others were keeping up with her pace – just. But she could not slow for fear of losing ground on the New Master of Darkness. On and on they journeyed, hours and hours passed, deeper into the darkness. Yet now and again Jesse saw flashes of luminosity, glimmers of mountain tops, or momentary light-filled woodlands. She was sure these were an illusion – either created by the Skaardrithadon or by her own mind, which sought relief from the fog in the familiarity of some imagined light. But the half-lit landscapes didn't diminish. They got stronger as the cloud thinned and faded.

At last, when she was on the brink of exhaustion, the fog lifted completely to reveal a land both bizarre and horrifying.

Jesse saw yellow scrubland as far as her eyes could see. There were rambling tracks of green verdant marshland, patchwork fields of dark lush forests, sweeping rivers and slashed sand banks. All of the land was stippled in a silver-blue light, like damp light on a November dusk. Here and there phosphorus grey streamers of mist hovered above ditches and dykes. Their waif-like shape bloomed and shrunk, forever changing. An over-riding smell of sulphur wafted from the marshland on a chilled breeze, as if many matches had been struck simultaneously. It was an unpleasant smell, but not over-powering. She blocked it from her mind and looked skyward. Flocks of bizarre two-headed, four-winged birds flew up from brown-banked waterless ditches, screaming, twisting, turning like a swarm of hungry locusts. In the far distance, massive dragon-like creatures lumbered across a tract of open scrubland, snorting, whistling an odd communication. One by one the great herd vanished into a forest. Then there was the eerie silence of this strange land, broken only by the odd whistle or snort. The birds and insects ceased their chittering. The breeze died, as the light started to fade. Black earth glimmered where a plough had turned the soil in the final vestiges of light. There was no sign of the vampire ploughman. And in between, the vast open plains were dominated by a yellow scrubland that grew darker and dimmer.

The Skaardrithadon was nowhere to be seen.

'Where are we?' Jesse asked.

Trondian-Yor had sped alongside. 'I'm not sure,' he said.

'Be a-tricking Iggywig thinks,' said the gobbit. 'And me be a-no liking it.'

'Are we still locked inside the Skaardrithadon's cloud?' asked Jesse.

'I fear the worst,' said Trondian-Yor.

'So do I fear the worstings.'

'What do you mean?' Jesse said.

'I think we are *inside* the Skaardrithadon's mind.'

'Are you sure?'

'It's highly likely,' Trondian-Yor said.

'How is that possible? This place looks and feels so real.' Jesse said.

'I don't know. It's just a feeling – a terrible feeling that we've been devoured somehow by his mind.'

'Devoured?'

18

'Eaten.'

'Eaten!'

'Ridiculous as it sounds, I think it has to be true.'

'No, it doesn't have to be true. And it is ridiculous. The whole idea of being eaten by someone else's mind is ... crazy.'

Trondian-Yor nodded. 'I know. But think about it. We entered the Skaardrithadon's cloud, his aura. His cloud is as much a part of him as your skin is a part of you, Jesse. If you look at your skin under a powerful microscope, what do you find?'

Jesse shrugged.

'You are the home of countless tiny creatures and life forms which are too small for the eye to see. Viruses are the smallest, averaging about one hundred nanometers, 100 billionths of a metre, in length.'

'That's small. So what are you saying?'

'I'm saying that we could be viruses to the Skaardrithadon's aura.'

'But that's impossible. We met him at the Innermost Sanctum. He was tall, but not *that* tall? He's no King Kong.'

Iggywig shrugged.

'We only met a part of him. His aura is vast.' Trondian-Yor said.

'But that was just cloud, wasn't it?'

'His cloud or his aura? It doesn't matter. It's the same thing. Think of him as a car that gives off exhaust fumes. How far do those fumes travel?'

'I don't know,' Jesse said. 'Miles probably.'

'Yes, probably. Do you see logic to my thinking?'

'A bit, but I'm still uncertain. It seems so incredible.'

'Just think how long we have travelled though. We've covered miles and miles inside his cloud.'

'Maybe we be a-going round in circles,' Iggywig said.

'Yes, maybe that's it,' Jesse said.

'Imagine if we were viruses on his skin.' Trondian-Yor carried on, unperturbed. 'How far do you think we would have travelled then?'

Jesse shrugged. 'This is too crazy to think about. My head is aching. Stop this now, please. Wherever we may or may not be, we still have the same goal, right?'

'Perigold,' the Dragon Hunter said.

'Exactly. And he's all that matters right now. We must search for the Skaardrithadon.'

'Yes,' said the Dragon Hunter. 'Where we find him, we will find Perigold.'

Jesse gazed at the wilted grass beneath her as they travelled on. It certainly looked real. Trondian-Yor had to be wrong. This wasn't the Skaardrithadon's mind or his skin, was it? If so, it was vast – a world that seemed extra-ordinarily vivid and real. No, this had to be a real world. And if so, where were they? What was this place called? Where was the Skaardrithadon?

So many questions unanswered.

'Look!' Kumo Diaz said. 'Up ahead. What is it?'

'Smoke.' Trondian-Yor said.

Jesse narrowed her eyes and watched the blue-grey smoke rise from a fire, which was blazing at the edge of a forest. At first, Jesse thought it was a bonfire or perhaps a campfire, but the closer she got to it, the more her horror grew. It wasn't a campfire or a bonfire. Now she saw the gaping jaws of an up-turned dragon, where tiny licks of fire flickered from leathery parted lips and where swirls of smoke billowed. The gigantic dragon groaned with each wheezing breath. It looked as if it might be sick or perhaps dying.

Landing a safe distance from it, Jesse transformed into her fairy self. She felt small and insignificant, less powerful, but definitely lighter and more nimble. These transformations are getting easier to do, she thought, stretching her arms and face muscles. Her skin felt tight, unlike her dragon self's skin (an armour-plating of scales really) which felt pliable and thick and very tough.

Now that she was close, she could see that the dragon was immense. Was it a Dragon? Lying marooned on its back, there were no spines visible. Its under-belly was covered in blue scales. With its four crocodile-like legs splayed, it looked vulnerable. It also looked so weak that one blow from the Dragon Hunter's sword and that would probably kill the creature. Its tail was twisted and barbed with small, curved red spines. So perhaps it was some kind of Dragon after all, she mused. But it was enormous. Jesse estimated from head to toe it must have been three hundred feet, the length of a full-sized football pitch.

She stepped in closer to its head where the fire and smoke spilled as if from a volcano with every wheezing breath. Its head was not one but two. They were attached to a pair of sinewy long necks, but each head was starkly different from the other. The head billowing smoke and fire was a dragon's head – no doubt. Its eyes were shut. Its nostrils opened and closed rapidly. It seemed unaware of their presence.

But the other head was rising up now to greet them. Like a cobra, red eyes fixed in a hypnotic glare, the head swayed from side to side. It was most definitely aware of them, poised ready to strike.

As Jesse eased back, the giant snake head matched her movement, rolling towards her. A thin black forked-tongue slithered from narrow lips. It tested the air, the scents of Jesse and her companions. It hissed menacingly.

'We mean you no harm,' Trondian-Yor said, almost in a whisper.

The snakehead lurked towards Trondian-Yor's voice. Could it see them? Jesse wondered. Was it blind?

Iggywig grabbed Jesse's arm and tugged her. She inched back, but her foot snagged a twig and the whiplash snap rang like a pistol shot.

The snakehead surged forward at her and stopped eighteen inches from her face.

'Stay still. Do not move,' the Dragon Hunter mouthed to Jesse.

She heard the buzz of his sword of light as he unleashed it from its scabbard.

The snakehead reared up. It had heard the buzzing sword, too.

Jesse held her breath, thinking about a transformation that could at least be as big as the gigantic creature. If it attacked would she be quick enough to evade it and transform? Could the Dragon Hunter stop it before it struck its fatal blow? Maybe, but she wasn't taking any chances. She saw in her mind's eyes exactly what she wanted to become. She wasn't sure if she could pull it off, but if it worked it might solve all of their current problems. Her transformation was smooth and effortless, like a gun sliding into a well-worn leather holster. Before the snakehead had time to react, Jesse emerged as a blast of wind. She wrapped herself around the snapping snakehead, chilled and air light. She entered its mind through its left nostril and sensed the world as the snakehead sensed it. Its world was a confusing place. It was injured, cursed, lost, lonely, and in terrible pain. It spat and struck out blindly at Jesse's companions. It was filled with terror, fearful for its life. Like liquid metal poured from a furnace, Jesse changed shape. Now she was a heat wave coursing through the creature's brain. She was more than Masdemdresa's wild wind gift she had inherited in the Skogsra Forest. Red, yellow, orange flame - only the flame was no longer solid. Like an insubstantial spider, it created countless, impossible tiny suns and planets, with vast spaces in between. It did not burn; it mended and healed like a needle and thread. The snakehead creature was reconnected to a future time or maybe a long distant past. It didn't matter – all that mattered was the reunion of mind and understanding.

When Jesse left the creature and retransformed into her fairy self, the snakehead opened its seeing eyes. It spoke in an ancient foreign tongue – sibilant, silky, smooth – that none could understand but Iggywig.

'What does it say?' Kumo Diaz asked.

'Thank you be its kind wordings.'

'Is that it?'

'It be a sleepy and a-needing a restings.'

'Is it part of the Skaardrithadon's cloud?'

'It be a-saying it does not be a-knowing what you be a-talking about.'

'It's unaware of the Skaardrithadon and his cloud?' Trondian-Yor said.

'Both be unknown. Creature be asking for a-restings.'

'What does it call this land?' Kumo Diaz said. 'It would be helpful to know. We need to get our bearings.'

Iggywig asked the question in the ancient creature's tongue. He frowned at its answer.

'Where are we?' Trondian-Yor said. 'Is this the Skaardrithadon's mind or not?'

'Yes, speak,' the Dragon Hunter said. He was concerned. He had seen a thin line of dark silhouettes etched along the horizon to the west.

Jesse glimpsed the concern in his face and followed his gaze. 'Trouble?'

The Dragon Hunter used his golden binocular eyes to zoom in on the silhouettes. They came sharply into view – hundreds of dark mottled creatures moving swiftly on foot. The Brood were closing in fast.

'Vile creatures.'

'How many?' Jesse said.

'Enough,' the Dragon Hunter said elusively.

'How many?' Jesse repeated with a harder edge to her voice. 'You do not need to feel that you are protecting me by hiding the truth. We need to know the odds.'

'Several hundred.'

'How far away are they?'

The Dragon Hunter looked at them for a minute or so, calculating. 'We have an hour at best, perhaps three-quarters of an hour at worst. They move quickly, but we have the advantage of flight.'

'Okay,' she said. 'We need ideas of what we do next.'

They discussed and made plans for their next move. It was a simple plan, but they really had little choice. The main thing was that they all agreed to the plan. There would be no turning back.

*

Kumo Diaz's ears pricked up. He stared at her with his one large eye. He wasn't surprised by Jesse's new authority. He had been watching her for a while now. Ever since she'd come back from the

24

dead, she'd changed. She was like two people. Sometimes she was the old Jesse, but most times she was the new domineering Jesse. He had taken note of her new powers and magic, and had detected her growing confidence with the new arts. It was a worry. She was more dangerous now than she'd ever been. But the tracker did not feel too panicked. He remained outwardly calm. The plan for her capture was, after all, still on-line and moving closer to success. Even though he knew it would not be easy – she was surrounded by much protection and magic – he was patient. If nothing else his wilderness training had taught him a great deal of patience. When the opportunity presented itself (as it always did on a hunt) he would take it. Then Jesse Jameson would be delivered alive with her precious golden glow intact.

Iggywig was still talking to the two-headed creature in its strange sibilant language.

'So does it know where we are?' Kumo Diaz said. His voice calm and normal.

'The creature be a-saying his species a-calling this land the Naargapire.'

'The Naargapire?' the Dragon Hunter said, lifting an eyebrow. He couldn't help the rising tone of his usually deep steady voice.

'Tis be as the creature says.'

'If this is the banished Naargapire, then we have travelled into the heart of the Skaardrithadon's homeland.'

'Yes, it makes sense,' said Trondian-Yor. 'Where better to lead us than his homeland?'

Jesse saw the glassy anxiety in the eyes of all her companions. 'What is so bad about the Naargapire?'

'Everything is bad in the Naargapire,' Trondian-Yor said. 'Believe me. This is the homeland of all the banished vampire races. From albino vampire bats, to the New Master of Darkness himself, they are all here. Every one of these creatures seeks blood. It doesn't matter what kind of blood. They will drink from the punctured arteries of common cattle. With equal delight they will drink the blood of human, fairy or a Caldazarian monster. It really doesn't matter to them. Each race's blood has its own taste, like the meat of a chicken or a cow or a pig.'

Jesse's brow furrowed. 'Hang on a minute. You said that all the creatures here were blood-sucking vampires.'

'Yes.'

'So where do they get their fresh supply of non-vampire blood?'

'Myth says that they have many ways of getting new blood. Riders stalk other kingdoms, seeking out easy targets. Sleeping children are a particular favourite. Sometimes they simply drink and the only signs they've visited a child's bedroom are the two holes in the unlucky victim's neck, and the nightmares which come night after night for years.'

'I thought that once a vampire had tasted your blood, you became a vampire, too,' Jesse said.

'It depends on the vampire's intent and its power of transformation.'

'Shape-shifting?'

'No, not shape-shifting. A select few – the Vampire Lords, the ruling class – have the ability to inject vampire DNA into a non-vampire's blood stream. As we know, the Skaardrithadon has done this to Perigold.'

'But why take Perigold?'

Kumo Diaz shrugged. 'We could speculate, but only the Skaardrithadon knows the reason why.'

'There are two basic effects of vampire DNA,'

Trondian-Yor continued. 'One is the out and out transformation to a full vampire. Memories of the victim's old self and life are erased. This seems to be the path chosen for Perigold. The Lord then moulds his new servant, trains him, instructing him in his full vampire ways and rituals. His loyalty to his new master is unfaltering.'

'And the other transformation?'

'That's a half-vampire state. A controlling venom is injected into the victim's blood stream. They retain their own identity without realising that they are being controlled by the Lord. This serves two purposes. One: the full vampires can drink the half vampire's blood when they are thirsty, or when their bloodlust has to be satisfied. Two: the half vampires' minds become pliable and easy to control. Distance is not a barrier. Full vampires – the Vampire Lords – can control the half vampires telepathically, visualising the task they want them to do. The majority of the creatures in the Naargapire are half vampires, who also feed on any blood they can. But...'

His voice trailed away.

'Yes?' Jesse said. She noted the fearful glimmer in his eyes. It worried her. She'd never seen Trondian-Yor like this before. He was typically so fearless and brave. 'Go on. What else?'

'Oh, it doesn't matter. It's just a myth, an idle rumour.'

'What rumour?'

'Yes, tis a-wise to be a-telling. Iggywig will be a-worrying now if not, kind wizard.'

He laughed dismissively. 'There's an ancient myth that tells of a hidden vault in the Naargapire. That's all.'

'And what's in the vault?'

'It doesn't matter. Really. I should have kept my big mouth shut.'

'Oh, come on, Trondian,' Jesse said firmly. 'You can't do this to us. We have a right to know what we are up against in this land.'

Trondian-Yor paused and scanned the horizon where the light was diminishing quickly. The silver-blue rays were changing to crimson and orange. It would soon be dark. In that darkness would come many vampires.

'The vault is said to be where the ancient Vampire Lords rest, in a kind of hibernation, waiting to be awoken by the Skaardrithadon. Legend says that he once led them into battle during the Fairy-Vampire Wars of long ago; that he is their undisputed leader. But no-one is certain. Stories change over time, become exaggerated. And in the retelling imagination adds and takes away many threads. We do not know the truth of the tales of the vampire vault. But if they are true, and the Skaardrithadon manages to find the vault and awaken the full vampire Lords who sleep there, then ...'

'Then what?'

Trondian-Yor shook his head slowly. 'It's unspeakable. I'm sorry. I have said too much already.'

'We are in great danger here,' the Dragon Hunter said. 'Our blood will attract much attention. We must move on.'

'Yes. We must keep moving,' said Trondian-Yor.

'Be a-place Iggywig no be a-caring for,' the gobbit said, staring at the two-headed monster he'd been talking to. The creature yawned. 'All creatures be a-drinking blood here.'

'Even this one?' Jesse said, nodding to the creature she'd healed.

'Yes.'

She backed away, even though the creature looked quite docile and harmless.

The two-headed creature yawned and settled itself down. It stretched out its great arms and legs. Its two heads rested on the ground, eyes closed. Within moments it was sleeping.

*

'What about Jake?' the Dragon Hunter said, placing the unconscious boy on the ground. 'Is there nothing you can do for him, wizard? He is slowing us down.'

Trondian-Yor knelt down beside Jake and put his hand on the boy's forehead. He felt hot and clammy. 'A fever is still with him.'

'Can you cool him?'

'Yes,' Trondian-Yor said. 'But he needs more than cooling.' He turned to Jesse. 'You have new powers Jesse. Perhaps you could use them?'

'Perhaps,' she whispered.

'What did you say?'

'Oh, nothing,' she said, a half-hearted smile twisted her face. 'I will try my best.'

Kumo Diaz watched her closely, fox-like.

Jesse crouched down next to Jake and stared at her fingers, trembling as she touched his head. She was waiting for the tingling sensation to arise in them, but nothing happened. She didn't feel self-assured, which was odd, because her mood-swings were beginning to worry her. One moment she felt very confident, able to focus her mind on the task ahead, but the next she felt hopeless and unsure. What if my powers have vanished? she thought. Couldn't they simply disappear? After all they came to me without warning. Maybe they will leave the same way? Perhaps they have left me?

All of a sudden, her fingertips started to tingle, an itchy kind of feeling that spread to her hands and arms. Then came the golden glow of her palms. She was not on fire, as Jake had claimed back in the Skaardrithadon's Innermost Sanctum. But a kind of magic fire burned and began its healing. Some other force took control, seemed to know instinctively what magic was needed. She did not transform into a healing wild wind or heat wave. A juddering static-like electricity jumped and zigzagged from her fingertips. It entered Jake's ears and nose and mouth. Within seconds he started to shake from head to toe, muscles stiffening. Slowly he rose from the ground, like a magician's trick of levitation. Yet this was no illusion.

Jake let out a grunt-cry. He whip-lashed his arms and legs as the purple-white electricity ran up and down the length of his body. It ran up and down for minutes, sizzling, seemingly frying his skin. But his flesh did not burn. His hair stood on end. His eyes snapped open and closed, showing white eyeballs. The sizzling light-show ceased. His skin was whiter than snow. His fingernails were on fire. His stiff body rose higher and higher, above the tree line. Electricity twisted like purple ropes around his face now, splitting strands, blooming out of his head like Medusa's hair. And all the time the twilight faded toward night.

Jesse's eyes snapped shut.

Jake sat up-right and screamed. He was a stiff L-shape, hovering high with electricity lassoed around him. Beneath him, Jesse's out-stretched arms pulsated rivers of thin light. They were attached as if by whipping electrical wires. Static charged the air and filled her companion's nostrils. That damp pungent after-the-rain smell was thick around them, clung to them, but there had been no rain.

Cut.

At first Jesse thought she heard the air whistling fast through her nostrils. But no, something invisible left Jake, scream-whistling across the scrubland. Like a snowball of fire and ice that *something* shot from his mouth and landed in a small stand of willows a score or more yards away. It left a blue smoke-trail which started from Jake's parted lips. He looked like a crest-fallen baby dragon, smoke drifting up from a mouth that had spat fire and ice.

Jake screamed, Jesse laughed.

Jake tumbled into the Dragon Hunter's comforting arms. Jesse stumbled into Kumo Diaz's arms, drained but elated. The tracker held her close, hiding his dark foxy smirk.

Three

Willow Wood

Jesse skipped over the giant sleeping creature's arrow-headed tail and ran confidently into the stand of trees. She ducked under whipping branches and willow withes, using her forearm as a shield. She did not fear these trees, as in the Skogsra Forest, where she and her companions had battled for their lives. These trees were rooted, deep and sucking moisture from the babbling nearby stream.

'Wait!' Trondian-Yor and the Dragon Hunter shouted in unison. They hurtled after her.

Jesse's speed did not slow until she saw the ball of fire and ice. The trees were closer now, and it was almost dark. The earth was covered in years of leaf-fall and each step was sometimes spongy and sometimes brittle. Half-rotted stumps loomed like slimy green skulls. She walked slowly through an overhang of willow withes, stopping a couple of feet from the fire and ice ball. Its flame was hot, very hot. It seared from its resting place at the base of a tree trunk. It had already charred black the bark.

'What are you doing?' Trondian-Yor said.

She turned to see him and the Dragon Hunter silhouetted darkly at the entrance of the willow tunnel. She could not see their faces. An extended twilight had come, held sway, held them all in some kind of light slippage.

'I want to see the thing that the witches had left inside Jake,' she said, turning towards the fireball. 'It has to be destroyed.'

'Yes, I agree. We must destroy it,' Trondian-Yor said, walking to her, 'but this new headstrong attitude you display could prove to be deadly for us all.'

'Headstrong?' Jesse's eyes twinkled. 'Me?'

'I have noticed it too,' the Dragon Hunter said. 'You are making decisions without us.'

'Am I?'

'You know you are,' Trondian-Yor said. 'Without consultation you could put all of us in great danger.'

'Could I?' Jesse couldn't hide her sarcastic tone. 'But I'm just a child. Surely a child couldn't do such a thing.'

'Stop it, Jesse,' Trondian-Yor said. 'You are more than a child, as well you know. You have returned from the dead. You have changed. Your powers are immense now – more than a child should have to bear. But the facts cannot be changed: your gift of the obsidian Seeing-Stone from the Elders of Elriad has become a part of you. The gift from Masdemdresa of the Wild Winds of Murokchi is a powerful force.'

'Oh, please,' Jesse said, glancing briefly at her firearm palm. 'Next you'll tell me that with these new powers come great responsibility. I must use them wisely, like a member of the Union of Thirteen would use them, that I need to learn patience and-'

'I see you mind read, too,' Trondian-Yor said.

Jesse caught the sadness in his words but chose to ignore it.

'I'm no mind reader,' she said flatly.

'Maybe not, but you would do well to listen to Trondian-Yor. We have all noticed your hostile attitude,' the Dragon Hunter said.

Jesse's laugh was a hollow shell. 'And you know all about being headstrong, Richard the Dragon Hunter, don't you?'

'Why do you call me Richard? You have never called me my given name before.'

Jesse shrugged. She didn't know. All she knew was that the remnants of the witches' spell had to be destroyed. All she cared for right now was Jake and Perigold. Time was running out. They must hurry – find the Skaardrithadon, reverse Perigold's vampire state. No! She must do those things. It was her responsibility. Trondian-Yor was right. She *was* responsible. She would make good the bad. She had the power now. She alone would-

'You will not go alone,' Trondian-Yor said, reading her mind. 'Perigold may well be your grandfather, but he is far more than that to many people.'

'I know,' she said. 'He's a member of your wonderful Union of Thirteen.'

'Jesse!' the Dragon Hunter shouted. 'Stop this!'

'Stop what?'

'Your disrespect and-' Trondian-Yor began.

'Independent thought?'

'No, not your own thoughts. Stop your arguing mind; stop your clever comments. Please. We are your friends.'

'I know – that's the problem.'

'What do you mean?' the Dragon Hunter said.

Jesse shrugged, stared at the fire and ice ball regretfully. Trondian-Yor and the Dragon Hunter withdrew out of Jesse's earshot behind a nearby tree trunk.

'She's afraid that she will lose us, like she feels she's lost Perigold,' the quargkin wizard whispered to the Dragon Hunter.

He nodded thoughtfully. 'Are you sure?'

'Yes. She has to cope with many things, so many changes, so many new responsibilities. She needs some time and space to think.'

'But we have no time. Jesse is right about Perigold. We must hurry before he becomes a vampire for ever.'

'Yes, Perigold is our number one priority. But we should watch Jesse closely. She has to find her own way, find her own balance inside.'

'But what if her headstrong attitude lands us in trouble?'

'Then we will have to deal with it as it happens. It won't be easy but what's new?'

The Dragon Hunter nodded. 'Jesse is a remarkable child. But she is still a child, and I am her guardian and protector.'

'Yes, you are a loyal and honourable friend. We will watch, support her as best we can.'

The Dragon Hunter and Trondian-Yor stepped out into the avenue of willows, and watched in amazement as Jesse leaned over the searing ice and fire ball. She picked it up in her hands and held it out to them.

'What do you suggest we do with it?' she said.

'What do you think?' Trondian-Yor said calmly.

'I have a plan for it.'

'A plan?' the Dragon Hunter said. He tried to keep his voice level and calm, but what in Boeron's name did she think she was doing? 'Never mind a plan. Drop it! Right now! Throw it away before it burns your flesh to cinders!'

'It's all right,' she said, smiling. She felt no pain. Her flesh did not burn. 'Its flames don't hurt me.'

'But how is that possible?' the Dragon Hunter said, wincing at what his mind thought should be happening: searing, smoking flesh and Jesse screaming.

She shrugged and smiled. 'Don't know. So do you want to hear my plan or not?'

'Please, go ahead. I'm listening.' Trondian-Yor said conversationally.

The Dragon Hunter continued to wince, rubbing his temple agitatedly. This child was remarkable.

Jesse told them her plan as they walked slowly along the avenue of willows, and they agreed. It was a good plan. They made preparations for the Driths who were probably following them. Leaving the ice and fire ball behind, the companions hurried on their way, following the faint, luminous trail the Skaardrithadon had left. And all around them, the vampire creatures of the Naargapire watched and waited patiently in the eerie twilight.

*

Kumo Diaz glanced at his fellow travellers and smirked beyond their gaze. Jake and the Dragon Hunter were riding on Cyren's tortoise shell back, with Iggywig and Trondian-Yor flying next to them. He was glad Jesse had let him ride on her Dragon transformation, glad the bond between them was growing stronger. When the time was right, he would strike. When he had gained her absolute confidence, he would make his move. The plan was perfect. The trap was primed and set. Patience, he urged.

He raised his mole-like snout and sniffed the pure, fresh sweet breeze of the Naargapire. It made his heart feel happier than ever to be here in this wilderness. In this wilderness alone, he would have been free from the interference of man, fairy or monster. Yes, he thought, this Naargapire wilderness is untamed and wild, unpolluted by greed and selfishness. This Naargapire is a tracker's paradise. And soon, I will be free to wander here till my dying days.

His one large fly-like eye scanned the terrain excitedly. Lush trees and dominant mountains, meandering rivers and curving hills, verdant valleys and steep gorges, vast untamed tracts of land loomed further than his far-seeing eye could capture. Herds of vampire beasts galloped below, on the open plains, flocks of vampire birds and bats showered the sky. It was a great untouched wilderness, a tracker's dream.

'Fly on, Jesse!' he yelled at her amidst the thumping beat of her enormous wings. 'We are gaining on the Skaardrithadon. Fly on!'

Kumo Diaz grunted his agreement. Fly on indeed, he thought. Hurry now.

Four

Incantations

The Driths emerged from the cloud screaming and swearing. The ghost sisters, Gwendrith and Dendrith, led the way followed by Kildrith and Jagdrith. On the young, blonde blind witch's shoulder sat an eagle owl. The creature's mind was controlled by the witch totally and she saw the world through the owl's eyes, too. A few dark wasps slipped in and out of the witch's mouth as if entering and exiting a hive.

'I smell them, not far away.' Kildrith said, sniffing the air like a wolf. 'East. Yes, they're heading east.'

'Are you certain, warlock?' Dendrith said. Her ghastly shimmering ghoul eyes flashed an ancient mistrust. 'Are you sure?'

'Yes. This way.'

'Why don't we send Clawdrith on ahead. She can track them down in silence, and I can see what she sees and tell you what-'

'We have no need for the bird.' Kildrith said abruptly. 'It's your pathetic attempt at making yourself seem useful. Let's face it. We all know the

38

gobbit outsmarted you with his Blinding Charm. You are a disgrace to Driths everywhere.'

Jagdrith's mucus-covered eyes rolled revoltingly in her head. Clawdrith flapped her giant wings. Her head twisted one hundred and eighty degrees and her eyes fixed glaringly on Kildrith. She attacked without warning, but the warlock's reflexes were quicker. He ducked and conjured a net, his wide-brimmed hat spinning like a plate from his head. The net caught the owl, banging her to the ground. She looked incredibly fragile, stranded. Her flapping wings were trapped, her feathers skewed in rope. Kildrith's filthy black boot heel came crashing down on the owl. But before bone-crunching contact was made, Dendrith unleashed a Paralysing Charm. Streams of ice poured from her fingertips. Like a malformed ballerina, Kildrith was frozen, his boot just inches from Clawdrith's neck. There was a sick frozen grin of pleasure creasing his ruined dark lips.

'Get the net off me!' Jagdrith bawled, flailing wildly like the owl.

'It's not on you, stupid,' Dendrith said.

'But it feels as though it's on me.'

'Well it's not. So stop acting like a baby. Get a grip!'

'Take it off! Get away!'

'Maybe Kildrith is right,' Dendrith said. 'Jagdrith is slow and stupid now. She holds us back.'

'Dearest sister,' Gwendrith said, with mock joy in her craggy eyes, 'I think your concerns are well-founded. Jagdrith is not only slow and stupid, she's pathetic and infantile.'

'But she is my daughter and you are her aunt.'

'True, sister dear.' Gwendrith's ghostly eyes widened. 'She's flesh and blood. We should help her understand the error of her ways.'

'Yes. She needs a lesson or two. But first we need to show her how sweet revenge can be.'

'Yes. Revenge.'

'East, then,' Dendrith said, and with a nonchalant wave of her ghostly hand she released both Kildrith and Clawdrith from their spells.

'Lead the way, warlock,' Gwendrith ordered. 'Let us save our hatred for the real enemy.'

Kildrith's nod was small and reluctant. He opened his body like a bat preparing for flight, but something bright caught his eye.

'What is it?' Dendrith said, following his gaze into the stand of willow trees.

'I'm not sure.'

'Imagination is a wonderful thing,' Jagdrith quipped.

'Shut it, blonde witch,' Kildrith said without looking at her.

'Hear how he speaks to me?' Jagdrith said. 'Isn't anyone going to rip out his disrespectful tongue?'

'Be quiet, daughter. Stop your whinging.'

'There,' said Gwendrith, pointing a thin ghost finger. 'Something burns amongst the trees.'

'Yes, I see it, sister. It feels familiar.'

'Familiar?'

'Yes, like a lost dog.'

'Very familiar.'

'Use your owl to find out what it is, child.'

Jagdrith sent Clawdrith into the Willow Wood.

'What do you see?' Gwendrith said.

'Trees,' Jagdrith said.

'What else?'

'Branches.'

'And?'

'Twigs.'

Dendrith's laugh was a hollow dead tree stump.

40

'Your daughter fools with me, sister,' Gwendrith said. 'Perhaps now would be a good time to help her understand the error of her ways.'

'Perhaps, sister dear,' Dendrith said. 'But she makes me laugh.'

'A blind buffoon – that's all we need.' Kildrith said under his breath.

'What did he say?' Jagdrith snarled. A couple of wasps spilled from her mouth. 'What did he say?'

'What do you see?' Gwendrith said.

Jagdrith saw the ice and fire ball through her owl's eyes, felt the dry heat from the impossible icy flame. Clawdrith landed on a branch a few feet above the ball, scanning the rest of the Willow Wood with sweeping turns of her head.

'Well, tell us.'

'It's the sleeping spell I clamped inside the male human child.'

'Impossible.'

'It's here. He's free. He's awake!'

'No! Unclamped? No – impossible.'

'The Skaardrithadon is in great danger again,' Dendrith said, an echo of fear on her lips.

'Yes, we must hurry more than ever. The Curse of Caldazar is alive again,' Gwendrith said.

'Two children together will chant the curse. The New Master of Darkness will be denied. Our revenge will be impossible to achieve without the Skaardrithadon's mighty powers,' Dendrith said.

She crouched down and opened her cloak. From the darkness she took out a small bronze bowl, decorated around the rim in Ancient Witch Glyphs. She placed it reverently on the earth and spat vile green globules of mucus into it. The mucus hit the inside edge. It was so thick and sticky that it didn't slide to the bottom of the bowl. It hung bat-like, defying gravity.

Dendrith slid her bony forefinger out and flicked the mucus with her dirty long fingernail into the bowl's bottom. She rubbed her thumb across her fingers and produced a few black beetle legs. Crushing them into a fine powder, she sprinkled them like sand into the bowl.

She chanted lines of harsh Ancient Witch Tongue and stirred the mixture with her forefinger. Sparks, tiny at first, ignited in the bowl. Then she added more spittle and a sprinkle of earth, pinched from the soil around. From her cloak she conjured powdered crow's claw, bat's wing, and snake's fang. She stirred absently.

'Something has slept here,' she said, noticing the large shallow dip in the ground all around them. See how flat the grass has become.'

'A resting hollow?' Gwendrith said. 'Are you sure?'

'Yes,' Dendrith said, tasting the air with her forked tongue. 'I am sure.'

'But the creature that rested here was massive.'

Dendrith nodded, re-focussing on her bowl of dark magic. She ignored the tremor in her sister's voice. 'Be watchful, sister. It may be close. The last thing we need right now is a surprise attack by a giant vampire.'

Gwendrith scanned the terrain and at last her eyes fell upon Jagdrith. 'What else do you see with your owl eyes?'

Jagdrith did not answer or move.

*

'Yes, that's it, come to me, sisters.'

She spat more thick mucus into the mixture. She stirred it with a scraping nail.

'We need you. That's right. We have deeds for you to do.'

She flicked a black dusting of crushed beetle's wings into the bowl. She stirred a little more, until the mixture resembled grey porridge.

'Come now from the deep. Awake. That's it. Come now, sister creatures.'

Red flames appeared from the mixture, licked the bowl. The light reflected menacingly in Dendrith's ghostly eyes. The mixture burned fiercely. A substantial acrid black smoke looped into the air, drifted into the witch's eyes and nose. It smelled like burning rubber tyres.

'Yes, come to me, sister creatures. I see you. Come now.'

From the flames came thousands of dark things – insects of sorts, a cross between a wasp and a locust. They poured as if smoke, wafting, formless, orange and black stripes. But when their smoking legs touched the soil of the Naargapire their forms stiffened, fleshed, boned, their veins and arteries coursing with life. They were six inches long – with large clear wings and sharp stingers. The upper half of their bodies, the head and thorax, resembled a locust. The lower half, the abdomen and stinger, was definitely wasp-like. They swam up in a great cloud, encircling the Willow Wood. The noise from their wings sounded like a squadron of planes. It was deafening. Round and round they flew, waiting for Dendrith to release them.

'This should give the brat Jameson something to think about,' Gwendrith shouted, trying to raise her voice above the din. 'Pure genius, sister. What do you plan? To sting her to death?'

'Something like that,' Dendrith said, and she waved the creatures away.

They swarmed off toward the east.

She turned to Jagdrith. She picked up the bronze

43

bowl and secreted it inside her cloak. 'So, the ball is your sleeping charm, is it not, daughter?'

Jagdrith did not answer.

'Do you hear me?'

Still no answer and no movement.

The blind fair-haired witch stood as still as a petrified tree trunk.

Kildrith strode over to her and clapped his hands in front of her face.

Jagdrith did not move.

'Counter charm,' he muttered, and ran into the Willow Wood.

'Damn that Jesse Jameson and her companions,' Dendrith screamed, now at her daughter's side. 'They will pay for this.'

'Is she dead?' Gwendrith said almost gleefully, hovering beside her sister.

'No. But she is close to it. She barely breathes.' She reached inside Jagdrith's chest with her ghost hand. 'Her hearts beat as slowly as a snail's heart.'

'Is there nothing we can do for her?'

'A counter charm, you mean?' She withdrew her hand from Jagdrith's chest.

'Maybe.' She glanced at the dimming horizon. Light was fading fast. 'But we must be on the move. We have to pick up their scent before they get too far ahead of us.'

'You have a counter charm, don't you?' Gwendrith said, smiling darkly.

'Yes. But I will not use it today. My stupid child needs a lesson or two. We will let her stew in the juices of this sleeping charm. Perhaps the nightmare experience will help her understand the true nature of a witch's hatred and spitefulness.'

'Perhaps,' Gwendrith cackled. 'Perhaps not.'

Kildrith emerged from the Willow Wood holding

44

the stiff sleeping owl. 'What should we do with this?'

'Carry it, and carry my daughter.' Dendrith's eyes narrowed. 'Harm a hair or feather and you will regret it.'

'I'll look after them both as if they were my very own,' Kildrith said ironically, tucking Jagdrith's petrified body under his arm like a roll of carpet. 'It'll be an honour. You know how much I adore animals and children.'

'Don't push your luck, warlock,' Dendrith snarled, floating to within an inch of him. She glared wildly into his eyes. 'I meant what I said. Harm a hair on my daughter's head and I'll slit your throat from ear to ear.'

'They are in safe hands, Dendrith,' he said, his unblinking eyes fixed like glue on her dark eyes.

'I doubt it,' Gwendrith said, joining them. 'You're so slimy that wet sand would slip through your hands.'

Kildrith ignored her. He knew he was no match for the ghost witch-sisters, but he would not show them any weakness. They reminded him of lionesses, after catching prey they no longer wanted. If he let them, they would toy with him until they became bored, and then they would kill him. Just like that. They would feel no pity or remorse. He stared straight through Dendrith, silent, waiting. His ruined face reflected in her pupils.

'They had better be safe,' Dendrith said at last.

'They will be.'

She turned with a flurry of dark cloak and knotted black hair, and glided away towards the distant mountain range in the east.

'What should we do with the ice and fire ball?' Gwendrith said, following her sister.

'Leave it.'

'Yes – good idea, sister dear. I like it.'

'How many do you think the ball will charm to sleep?'

'It depends how long it's active,' Kildrith said conversationally, bringing up the rear. 'A day may bring a couple of sleeping creatures – a month a lot more.'

'Shut it, warlock,' Gwendrith snapped. 'Shut your clever blabbering mouth. If we want your opinion, then we'll ask for it, won't we, sister dear?'

'We have company,' Dendrith said, gliding to a halt. 'Look behind us.'

The two-headed creature appeared from its hiding place, – a small hill just beyond the Willow Wood.

The creature was enormous, dwarfing the wood. But it was not the one Jesse had healed. This creature was taller and broader, and had rusty black iron scales and one dragon head which puffed great plumes of acrid black smoke. Its second head was a snakehead, and the creature's slow deliberate steps crashed the ground like an earth quake.

'What is it?' Gwendrith said, moving behind her sister for protection.

'A Megadon,' Dendrith said. 'Let's go.'

'Run?' Kildrith couldn't hide his surprise. 'Afraid to stand and fight?'

Dendrith quickened her pace. 'Where there is one Megadon, there will be many. They are ancient herding creatures, but they are not sheep. They hunt in packs like wolves. We are no match with or without our magic.'

'But we are dead. How can they hurt us?'

'This is the Naargapire. Our deaths mean nothing here.'

'Are they vampires?' Gwendrith said.

'Of course they're vampires,' Kildrith said acidly.

'This is the Naargapire, you dumb witch. What did you expect? Mermaids? Next you'll be asking if their bites hurt and their venom curdles the blood in your veins!'

'Watch your mouth, warlock,' Gwendrith said. 'Watch your blabbering big mouth.'

'Or you'll do what?'

Gwendrith made to lunge at him, but Dendrith stepped in her way. 'Cut it out, the pair of you. We have bigger problems than your infantile banter. Look.'

Dozens of Megadons were stomping out of their hiding places all around them. In less than a minute the Driths were surrounded by hundreds of the creatures. Froth and green drool dripped from their mouths in thick sticky drops. Thin long forked-tongues tasted the air. Their hooded eyelids blinked slowly over dark glaring eyes.

'Let's get away from here,' Gwendrith said, her voice quivering.

The circle of deadly Megadons closed in.

'Now!'

The Megadons stampeded, dust and galloping hooves and roars and hisses filled the Driths' ears with deafening noise.

Dendrith flew straight up into the air like a rocket, cursing the creatures far below. Gwendrith matched her move, as did Kildrith, who was still clutching the petrified owl and Jagdrith. When the herd of Megadons were mere specks beneath them, Dendrith glided towards the east, with Gwendrith and Kildrith arguing and insulting one another.

Dendrith ignored them, focusing her witch vision far ahead to distant mountains. She could hear the New Master of Darkness calling her on, guiding her even closer to Jesse Jameson. Dark evil thoughts raced in her mind. She quickened her speed, muttering curses and rehearsing black malicious charms. This time she would extract the fairy child's golden glow. Once the swarming insects had caught and paralysed her, she would take what was hers. Though she knew she would never be flesh and blood again, she would still be able to use the golden glow for her own wicked purposes. Once she'd gained entry to the human world, she would feed on the golden glows of more children, becoming a witch-ghost of immense power. But she wouldn't tell the others about her ambitions. Even her sister was spiteful enough to snatch the glow for herself. Secret, hidden, mine.

Five

The Doers

The ruined yellow-stone village sat a few miles away on top of the rise of the hill. Behind it, the far-away jagged mountain peaks of snow shimmered like some distant prize. Even though they'd headed towards the mountains for hours, they didn't seem to be getting much closer. Jesse thought again that Kumo Diaz's estimate of the distance between the Willow Wood and the mountains was hopeless. Even odder – the thin shroud of twilight still clung everywhere. Night time hadn't come yet.

'Why are the mountains just as far away as when we left the Willow Wood?' she asked with her deep dragon voice. Her huge wings flapped slowly, a measured beat of enormous power. She was flying just above the tree line of a vast pine forest. The sweet smell of pine sap was everywhere.

Kumo Diaz shifted uneasily on Jesse's back.

'I don't know,' he said. He spoke the truth.

'Do you think they are an illusion?'

'Like a desert mirage?'

'No, not like a mirage. Magic, a charm, a shape-

49

shifting giant creature out there playing games?'

'The Skaardrithadon, you mean?'

'Maybe.'

'Anything is possible. The lands of Naargapire are magical, wild, unpredictable. That's why I love them so much.'

'You sound as if you have been here before?'

'No,' Kumo Diaz lied. 'I have never been here before.'

'So why do you love them, speak as if you know the Naargapire well?'

'I have read many of the ancient stories, myths, legends – that kind of thing.'

'Right,' Jesse said, nodding. Her mind flashed back to her obsession with a book about myths and legends. It seemed such a long time ago since she'd sat in detention at St. Wormdirt's, poring over it, discovering so much about fairy folklore. She could appreciate Kumo Diaz's fascination.

'I have heard many great and heroic legends from the Story Telling Rooms of Finnigull,' the tracker continued.

Jesse's mind flashed back to Kayblade's spooky Story Telling Room in Alisbad. She hadn't cared for the maze of dark corridors much.

'The vampire creatures of the Naargapire are misunderstood,' Kumo Diaz said, disguising his words to make them sound as casual as he could, but feeling passionate about the misunderstood vampires. He didn't want to sound like an adult giving a child a lecture. He needed to befriend Jesse, not alienate her.

'How are they misunderstood?'

He smiled behind her back. That's it, Jesse Jameson, he thought. Keep biting at the worm with your questions. He saw himself as a fisherman, his words were his bait. Once she'd been hooked, he'd reel her in. 'You wouldn't understand,' he said at last.

'Why wouldn't I understand?'

His smile widened. He could that feel she was about to bite. 'You are a fairy.'

'And what difference does that make?'

'A lot when talking about the Fairy-Vampire Wars.'

'Try me, I might surprise you.'

Hooked. Now reel her in.

'You know about the Fairy-Vampire Wars, don't you?'

'A little. Tell me more.'

'It was a long bloody war that killed too many creatures on both sides. Officially the Storytellers talk about all kinds of things you'd expect a war to be about.'

Keep reeling.

'Land? Power? Greed? Freedom?'

'Yes, and more,' he said. 'Revenge for relatives lost in battle. Many wars are continued because loved ones have been killed. The relatives who carry on fighting desperately want revenge for a sister's death, or a grandfather's death, or a great grandmother's death. Creatures of all species find it hard to let go of the past, the memory, and what others before their time did to their own flesh and blood. The Fairy-Vampire Wars were just like many other wars in that respect.'

Jesse thought about the human wars that she knew about. She had studied World War II at school as part of the class History topic. Satellite TV had brought the Iraq and Palestine conflicts into her home. Unlike Jake, who couldn't bear to watch the news of war, she would force herself to watch.

Strange, she knew, but that's the way it was for her. She wasn't sure why she was fascinated. But she didn't leave the room, or turn off the TV as Jake always did, until the bad news had been read. Afterwards, she felt very lucky to live in a country free from war.

'I want to know what's happening in the world,' she would say to Jake. 'Sick,' was his usual reply, and he'd stomp off to play fighting games on his Playstation.

'It is awful what people do to one another,' she said at last to Kumo Diaz. Her wings beat steadily, like the hands of a flapping clock.

'Yes – it is. And the saddest thing of all is that each side believes that their actions are right.'

'The saddest thing is all the pain and suffering,' Jesse said. 'Why can't people let go of the past? Start again?'

Reeling her in a little more.

'Memory. It's like a trap. It grips with teeth as sharp as needles.'

'Then we'd all be better off without memory,' Jesse said indignantly. 'Wouldn't we?'

'I don't know, Jesse,' Kumo Diaz said. 'Memory is a wonderful thing in many ways. Think of all the good times.'

Jesse nodded. 'Good and bad times. Memory keeps them all. The mind is a complex thing.'

'Yes, and wars are complex things, too.'

'Killing people isn't complex. A single bullet will do,' Jesse said harshly.

'You speak wisely for one so young,' Kumo Diaz said. 'But believe me, wars are not simple things.'

'Perhaps not, but stopping them could be *so* simple. If everyone refused to fight in them, then there'd be no wars.'

Kumo Diaz laughed. 'Only a child's mind could make life so simple. Adults think differently, unfortunately. Adult life is a complex thing.'

'Yes, I am beginning to understand that. It worries me.'

'In what way?'

'It worries me that I'm going to grow up and turn out exactly the same.'

'You'll never be the same, Jesse Jameson.'

'Why do you say that?'

'Because you are already as different as different can be.'

'My magical gifts, you mean?'

'Yes. You are a remarkable child.'

'But that's just it. I don't want to be remarkable. I want to be normal.'

'Why?'

'Because I miss the simple things I used to have in my life. I was so free then. I had no responsibilities. I was just an average kid, doing average things. It was great.'

'I understand,' the tracker said. 'You've been robbed of your childhood.'

'Yes, that's it. I've been robbed.'

'And who robbed you, Jesse?'

She had the briefest of moments to consider that question, and what she discovered really disturbed her. It sent an unbearable aching pain to her hearts. The truth of who was responsible for robbing her of her normal childhood was too horrible to think about. She shoved the horror to the back of her mind. For the moment, there were more pressing concerns.

*

Trondian-Yor was the first to hear the swarm of insects. He turned and pointed to the blob in the distant sky. Jesse's dragon ears heard it next. It was like the dull drone of a squadron of planes. She turned and stared at the mesmerising sight.

'Tis not a good omen,' Iggywig said. 'What be that a-buzzing cloud?'

The Dragon Hunter narrowed his golden binocular eyes. He zoomed in, magnifying the dark blob. He saw them clearly. 'Wasps or bees,' he said. 'Thousands of them.'

'We must hide,' Jesse said.

'Not fight?' the Dragon Hunter said.

'No,' she said. 'I think we should avoid them, don't you, Trondian-Yor?'

'Yes, that's very sensible, Jesse.'

'If we quicken our pace, we should be able to out run them.' Kumo Diaz said. 'The village is not far.'

'Very well,' the Dragon Hunter said. 'But let's hurry.' He was looking back over his shoulder again. 'The insects are gaining on us. They are very fast.'

*

They arrived at the village a few minutes later. Wild ragged clouds and a bitter halting wind rose up from the deserted village, tearing at Jesse's cheeks. The twilight had not diminished. A half moon had appeared low on the horizon. There were possibly twenty-five buildings huddled either side of one wide road. That was it – except a grave yard on the outskirts, its tombstones twisted, sunken, green with age. Slants of sharp silver-blue moonlight glimmered from a pair of bell towers below. A single deep bell tolled in the wind. The second belfry was empty, but crouched low where the bell should have been, Jesse saw a frightening sight. It was an enormous bat.

'It's huge,' she said. 'Is it a vampire?'

'All creatures in the Naargapire are vampires or

soon become them,' Kumo Diaz said. 'It's only a matter of time. Sooner or later it'll happen to all of us.'

'How can you say that? It sounds as if you *want* to become a vampire.'

Kumo Diaz's single eye showed no sign of emotion either way. He knew he could have made Jesse's descent onto the ochre rock hard street below treacherous, deadly even. There were many things he could have done if he'd unsheathed his hunting knife whilst on her back. But he thought that that was where it was all going to end for Jesse Jameson and her companions. Once the transformational vampire blood coursed through their veins from the giant bat-guardian's fanged teeth then his part of the job would be over. His Naargapire dream was about to begin: free passage as a non-vampire tracker throughout the Naargapire.

Seconds before Jesse touched down on the dusty street, the Dragon Hunter launched himself from Cyren's back with the agility of a gymnast leaping over a wooden horse. He hit the ground and rolled over onto his feet, unleashing his sword of light. It buzzed menacingly.

The giant bat dropped into a silent eerie glide. It flapped its wings quickly half a dozen times, gaining speed fast.

'Come feel the pain of light,' he said, knees bent, two hands gripping the sword's hilt.

The giant bat evaded the Dragon Hunter's two strikes with silky ease. It flew up and landed under the eve of a red roof stone temple. It was the only eve that could hold its considerable weight and giant size in the village.

'Is that the best you can do?' the Dragon Hunter scoffed.

The bat's tiny eyes glistened like black polished rock. Its wings were folded close to its narrow body. It clung to the eve of the roof upside down, waiting. The wind howled through the shuttered windows of the temple's façade. The distant hum of the swarm of insects was growing louder and louder.

Jesse transformed into her fairy self and stood beside Jake, who'd dismounted Cyren and was stretching his stiff arms and legs.

'It's not wise to stray out into the open,' Trondian-Yor said, landing next to them. 'Let's get inside.'

'Tis a wise wordings, kind wizard,' Iggywig said, hovering a few feet above the street. 'This batty vampire be a-giving Iggywig the willies.'

Jake laughed, Jesse nodded.

'Good idea – let's get off the street,' she said.

'But what about the bat?' Kumo Diaz said.

'What about it?' Jesse said, leading them across the street towards a row of deserted yellow-stone terraced buildings.

'She's right,' Trondian-Yor said. 'The bat's no problem for the moment.'

'Shame,' the Dragon Hunter said, still crouched in a defensive stance, sword buzzing. He saw a cloaked and hooded figure slip quickly through the temple's double doors.

The bat did not move, but it did not stop watching them for a single moment.

*

Jesse paused at the door that hung weathered and rotten, glancing up at the giant bat. Something passed between them, a signal, a thought, perhaps a sonar bleep too high to hear with her fairy ears. There was sadness, a reluctance to guard the ruined village, a sense of duty and honour at being chosen … by … the …

A vision flashed into her mind like a flash of sheet lightning. It came and went in a millisecond, but left vibrant distinct impressions. The cold, calculating eyes of the Skaardrithadon lit up in the darkness of her mind. She shuddered, held the base of her skull where a surging ache now pounded. Fangs dripping with rose red blood ... a pale white neck punctured with two holes, cold eyes, needled-sharp fangs, smooth soft neck ...

'Trap!' Jesse yelled, staggering forward, arms splayed zombie-like in front of her to cushion the fall. She crashed through the rotten door, which splintered at the edges and squealed open. She collapsed onto her knees just inside the threshold, breathing heavily.

'What is it, Jesse?' Jake said, dropping to the floor beside her.

Jesse couldn't speak. Her voice was stuck in the back of her parched throat.

'Tell me. What is it?' Jake repeated. He shook her by her shoulders.

She turned slowly, dazed, eyes wide with terror. She looked like a rabid wild dog, running her fingers through her hair, stretching the flesh of her forehead back so that her eyes widened even more. 'It's a trap. The Skaardrithadon has led us here. Get out of this town!'

The Dragon Hunter ran over to the doorway from his position in the street. Dust squirted up behind each footfall, swirling like dull yellow clouds on the wind. The silver-blue moonlight etched momentarily an expression of dark fear on his gaunt face. He turned his head to look across the street to where the giant bat hung, motionless. He'd half expected it to swoop down as he ran with his back turned; half expected it to strike a coward's blow. But it did not.

It must have some honour within its heart, he thought. This notion was a little comforting to him, to his warrior mind. A little but not much. He didn't care for the watching and waiting game it played. But that, at least, was over and done with for now.

He turned to Cyren, who was much too large to fit into any of the doorways, and motioned for the creature to fly out of harm's way. With great lurching strides, Cyren galloped along the main street, flapping his enormous wings, slowly rising into the air.

'Get in!' the Dragon Hunter yelled.

'Get out!' Jesse shouted.

The Dragon Hunter hauled Jesse to her feet and dragged her deeper into the darkness. The others followed, slamming the rickety half broken door behind them.

Thin beams of dusty blue moonlight broke through the cracks and holes in the door and partially illuminated the room. It was small. Its plaster walls were cracked and crumbling, floorboards rotten and splintered. It looked as though it was about to cave-in.

'We have to get out of this town,' Jesse repeated again. 'I've had a vision. I saw him, the Skaardrithadon. He's led us into a trap.'

'Most probably. But we go nowhere,' the Dragon Hunter said. 'Look.'

Jesse walked carefully across the rotten floorboards and squinted through one of many tiny peepholes which riddled the window shutters. The village street was crawling with pale people – humans. Some had broken into small gangs and were searching the buildings as they went by. But most of them were making their way toward the terraced buildings. They would soon find them.

'Look at the holes in their necks,' Trondian-Yor said. 'The mark of a vampire.'

'But they're human?' Jesse said, surprised.

'The Naargapire is the homeland of many vampires – goblins, trolls, nuggies, hunky punks, elves, humans and many more races.'

'How is that possible?'

'Riders, the vampire army, have one mission: enter all the dimensions, lands, and kingdoms and harvest non-vampires. Those who've become vampires without a fight fair better than the creatures reluctant to feel the blood-suckers' bite. These human vampires work for the Skaardrithadon, no doubt, but look at their clothes. They are not modern. These people are old vampires; they are from a long time ago. Possibly hundreds of years old. Willing servants. Willing Doers.'

'Doers?'

'They get things done for the Skaardrithadon. Mostly they live in towns and villages, seem almost normal. But they are not. They feed on blood, but also eat other food, solids such as meat and vegetables. They are half-vampires. The venom injected into their blood keeps them docile and obedient. But they have to be blooded by the full vampires regularly.'

'What does blooded mean?' Jesse said, although she had a good idea of its meaning.

'The full vampires drink the Doers' blood from time to time to satisfy their own bloodlust and to re-inject the controlling venom.'

'They sound as if they have been drugged,' the Dragon Hunter said, his voice thick with disgust.

'Yes. In a way, it is true. Those half-vampires are drugged I suppose. But part of their brain works independently from the Lord, unlike full vampire slaves such as Perigold is becoming. Perigold will be under the total control of the Skaardrithadon. Once the full vampire conversion is complete, then the Perigold who we know will not exist.'

'But there are children out there,' Jesse said, noting the staring, unblinking wildness in their beady dark eyes that filled her with anxiety.

'Young, old, male, female. It makes no difference. The Skaardrithadon takes them all – his Riders have no preference and harvest every non-vampire they can find.'

'That's terrible.'

'Yes. It is. And now his Doers come to drink from our blood.'

Jesse stepped away from the window and turned into the twilight. Her companions were gathered around her, waiting.

'Shall we fight or run?' Kumo Diaz said.

Jesse's face was full of surprise. They were looking at her, waiting for her to make the decision. It was a life-threatening decision; but simple, when she thought about it.

The door heaved on its hinges. Splinters cascaded like wooden drops of rain onto the floor. Another blow and it would shear off completely.

'Run or fight?' the Dragon Hunter said.

Trondian-Yor looked anxiously toward the cracking door.

'Well?'

Jesse Jameson opened her mouth to speak-

The door crashed off its hinges and fell with a slapping shudder. Dust puffed up and filled the entrance briefly. As it settled and cleared, Jesse saw the Doers clambering to get to her companions. They were out numbered by twenty to one. Men, women, and children snarled, raised clawed hands, foamed white spittle, exposing fangs. They came for them screaming in high-pitched squeals, came for them in a wave of bloodlust.

'Run!'

Jesse twisted around and hurtled into the kitchen. Startled rats squealed and fled into crannies and crevices, leapt into the darkness of the holes which littered the rotten floorboards. The window was boarded up, and the backdoor was locked. Jesse tugged on the handle but it wouldn't budge. She glanced over her shoulder to see the first Doer entering the kitchen. He was an old man. He had big callous hands. They were hooked into claw-shapes. His thick white hair bristled with anticipation. He was crouching low. He looked like a wolf about to bring down its prey.

The Dragon Hunter pushed her aside. He reduced the door to kindling with a single blow from his sword of light, and as the Doer sprang wolf-like at them, the Dragon Hunter dispatched him with a single blow. He screamed and collapsed in a heap as they stepped out into the overcast silver-grey moonlight. The wind whipped them bitterly. A storm was brewing. The air smelled of rain and lightning.

Jesse hurried down a narrow alley, flanked by high leaning stone walls. The Doers were a few yards behind them, running now. Even the old people ran as if they were young. They were fit and fast, with crazy staring unblinking eyes.

'We can't out run them,' the Dragon Hunter said. 'Let's make a stand and fight!'

At the far end of the alley, more Doers charged around the corner. Jesse and her companions were running straight at them. They were trapped. She tried to block the memory of her vision: cold eyes ... needle-shape fangs ... smooth soft neck.

61

'Fly!' Trondian-Yor said, bringing them to their senses. 'Fly!'

Jesse transformed into her dragon self, grabbing Kumo Diaz with her talons, soaring up above the village. She glanced down and saw Cyren landing around the corner from the main street. He hit the dirt with a mighty thump and skidded a few feet along the street. A great cloud of yellow dust mushroomed around him. He lumbered left into the alley.

Jake saw him and ran with all his strength toward the creature. He jumped on Cyren's back, urging him to fly.

Cyren waited. One of them was missing.

It was the Dragon Hunter. He drew his sword of light, splayed his legs in an attacking posture.

'Don't be a fool!' Trondian-Yor shouted. He and Iggywig were already hovering out of range of the Doers. 'Climb on Cyren!'

Jesse couldn't believe her eyes. The Dragon Hunter was waving Cyren away, wading into the vampire mob, slashing and hacking. Cyren took off, knocking a dozen or so Doers out of his way with his great swishing tail.

'No!' Jesse screamed, flipping Kumo Diaz onto her back. She descended like a hawk to help the Dragon Hunter.

But the Dragon Hunter didn't seem to hear her. His eyes were locked on the multitude around him. He had flipped to that mind space where determination and adrenaline had taken control. Had Jesse been able to see his eyes, she would have seen the glassy expression of a warrior fighting instinctively without thought or feeling. For better or worse, he was on his own now. He had become a killing machine.

He hacked his way through the Doers who'd rounded the corner, running, leaping over bodies as they fell. His footfalls raised clouds of hanging yellow dust. The moon disappeared briefly behind a filthy dark bank of clouds. He skipped over more falling bodies, and still they came, howling and screaming for his blood. But now they brandished knives and axes of their own. They slashed out at him, but his reflexes were razor-sharp. He was the Dragon Hunter, slayer of many fearsome beasts. He had spent many years honing his skills with a sword. His attack and defence moves were silky smooth. He ducked and parried, wove and side-stepped the oncoming blows. And still more Doers poured out from the buildings all around him, intent on harming him. They were determined to take him down.

'Stop this madness!' Jesse roared, swooping down to make a grab for him. He waved her away. 'What are you doing?'

The Dragon Hunter did not answer.

In the diffused moonlight, he barged his way around the corner and into the main street. The moon peeped out from behind a veil of thin cloud, vanished, then appeared again fully, casting a silvery-blue light on them. Hundreds of Doers came now, sprinting out from doorways.

He ran and they followed, as if he was the Pied Piper, across the street and toward the temple. Thickening clouds of dust spumed up around them. They coughed and spluttered, and drove on toward him. He leapt onto the cracked pavement, slipped, regained his footing. He felt claws dig into his back through narrow gaps of his lower armour. A hand gripped the top of his thigh as if a vice. He twisted around, shaking them off. He felled the three young

63

Doers who had been snarling at his back. He ducked into the open doorway, not looking up at the giant bat hanging beneath the eve. Something unseen passed between them: voices, visions, sensations. He shook them off, too, re-focusing his golden eyes on the dim, candle lit interior of the temple. His footfalls echoed and slapped. He turned to slash another Doer, but discovered that he was alone in the semi-darkness. He could see the Doers crowded outside the door, snarling, baying for his blood. For some reason, they did not enter.

*

The insects came down on them in a great eddying swarm of black and orange. They did not strike instantly, but seemed to be considering their next move. Then without warning they all attacked Jesse's dragon head. Even though Kumo Diaz sat astride her back, they ignored him totally.

Jesse did not panic. Her mind whirled, a creative carousel of possibilities opening before her. She could feel the Seeing-Stone guiding her. There were options – many. She chose one quickly. Her head had become a mass of wings and stingers. But instead of overwhelming her, something else was happening as they stung her relentlessly. She transformed her jaws into an enormous maw, so wide that it swallowed them whole in one great belching gulp. Seconds later, she fried them with blasts of dragon fire. They screamed as they died. Her head morphed to its original dragon size, as she spat out the charred cinders of the insects. They showered down like ash-rain onto the temple below.

Six

The Temple

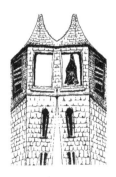

One of the Doers, an elder judging from the tint of his grey hair, leaned forward, reached out. He grabbed hold of the handle. A demonic grin twisted his thin black lips.

The door slammed shut, reverberating around the high hollow temple. Something moved amongst the pews. Slithered, crawled with speed behind the altar. It was thin and long by the sound of its motion. It was also far enough away from him to be of no immediate danger. He put it to the back of his mind for a moment. He needed to get his bearings. He needed to catch his breath.

Breathing in huge gulps, he came to a stand-still and surveyed the temple. It was more like a cathedral, he now noticed. There were pillars and vaulted ceilings with round arches. The walls had small candle-lit alcoves sunken into them. The candle light flickered, casting long deep shadows. Somewhere, a hundred steps or more ahead, there burned sweet-smelling incense. He walked slowly along the aisle toward the altar, scanning the dark recesses with his extraordinary eyes. He listened to his own breathing, shallow now, and then held his breath, stopping, listening. His own blood raced into his heart like a dam bursting its banks. He could hear it pounding in his ears. His throat was parched. He licked dry lips with his dry tongue. He needed a drink. All that was in this place was probably just holy water. That would do. He wasn't fussy. He would drink whatever he could find. He listened carefully again. No-one stirred, but he knew he was not alone. Whatever lurked in the dark places was watching him, waiting.

He walked on toward the altar and the smell of sickly sweet burning incense. Outside the mob were silent. Inside he now felt his own heart thumping in his chest like a drum of war. He had his breathing under control, but his heart raced on. He raised his sword of light with two hands in front of him. It purred softly.

Step twenty two.

He edged closer to the altar. His steps were slow and measured, light steps taken on the tips of his toes almost. He was sure that something or someone was hiding behind the block of stone to his right. Yes, something thin and tall. It was still now, but waiting for its chance to make its move.

Step twenty six.

The marble floor beneath him squeaked slightly as he walked. He tried to change his step to reduce the give-away sound. There, that's better, he thought. Noiseless. Well, almost.

He shuddered. The chill of the temple seemed to want to freeze his flesh. It wrapped around his legs and numbed his fingers. It was bitterly cold.

He continued to walk slow, measured strides, eyes fixed on the altar and what lay hidden behind it. He also looked sideways at the same time, out of the periphery of his vision. He was searching for the slightest movement. His temples ached with a dull thud. His neck muscles tightened like ropes holding a mainsail in a raging storm. He tried to slow down his breathing even more, relax his shoulders, but he was wound up tighter than a drum skin parched by a desert sun.

Step thirty nine.

He felt giddy and sick in the pit of his stomach. Each step echoed somewhat even though he had eliminated the annoying squeak that gave away his position. His clothes rustled as he moved. He was exposed, vulnerable, and very alone. His sword buzzed reassuringly as he tilted it forward forty five degrees in anticipation of attack. Why was he so intent on walking quietly, when his noisy sword gave away so much?

Step forty five.

His mind wandered to Jesse high in the sky and his heart sank. *Protector and guardian in this world and the next?* That's what he'd told her on several occasions, hadn't he? *I am your protector and guardian in this world and the next.* He shook his head and grunted his irony. *What are you doing?* she had shouted. He wasn't sure, but he was sick of running – he was always on the run just lately. It twisted deep, like a steel blade into his gut. He was not a runner, a chicken, a yellow-bellied coward. No, sir, he was not. He was a warrior, a soldier, a hunter. It was time to fight.

Step sixty.

He glimpsed the row of thick stubby candles flickering on the altar. He estimated, his mind on edge, weighing up the odds, calculating the risks, the pros and the cons. A light breeze whipped up around his ankles, blew out a few candles, but he didn't seem to notice. He should have noticed. It was a bad sign.

Locked on the altar, he continued forward.

Step sixty five.

What was he doing? Jesse's protector and guardian had gone A.W.O.L. This was madness and *so* irresponsible. In the far corner he could see steps which he knew led high into the temple's tower. Couldn't he turn away and climb the steps? Once he'd reached the top, he could signal, shout for help. Jesse could fly down and rescue him from there. He would be reunited – guardian and protector back fulfilling his duty.

Step seventy three.

He heard something move to his right behind him, but he still kept walking. It was too far away to pose an immediate threat.

Three more candles blew out on the altar, leaving just two alight. He tried to ignore the beads of sweat trickling down his face and the tackiness of his hands. His temples thumped a massive painful headache. His legs stiffened. It felt as if he was walking on wooden stilts.

Step eighty one.

Almost there now.

What lurked behind the altar did not move, did not spring its attack. He was certain it was the Skaardrithadon.

You have nerve and patience, the Dragon Hunter thought of the Skaardrithadon, but soon you will be dead. He moved his sword in a blazing arc before him with confidence and childish glee. He thought again what he had thought many times in the electric moments before battle: I am a warrior. I may die fighting, but my death will be noble. I chose to be here. No-one else chose for me. I am a warrior. I am free to fight or walk away. I choose to fight.

Step eighty nine.

Just eleven more steps.

Run! Run toward it! Now! Take whatever skulks behind the altar *before* it takes you! His mind raced with the panic that came and went just before the first blow. Crazy thoughts came in those moments. His adrenaline had already kicked in and his fight or take flight instincts had taken over – almost. He still managed to retain control – just. He would not run anymore. Not today. It was now or never. He would fight. If the Skaardrithadon waited for him behind the altar, then so be it! I have him in my sights! I am the Dragon Hunter. You will know my name by the pain of my blade.

Step ninety one.

Nine steps ... eight ... seven ... six ...

His mind slipped into strange thoughts.

The giant bat's silent communication loomed large in his mind. Fangs, blood, punctured neck ... service to the Skaardrithadon. Is this where I am headed? He saw himself turn, as if in a dream. Just two steps from the altar, his mind opened and visions entered. He was back at the temple's entrance. He opened the door and light blinded him momentarily. He was met by hundreds of Doers, pouring out of every building onto the dusty yellow moonlit street. They circled him like a pack of hungry wolves, preparing to strike, closing-in for the kill.

The Dragon Hunter stood motionless and looked up at the giant bat still roosting under the eve of the temple. Something passed between them. The Dragon Hunter obediently nodded his understanding and sank to his knees, tossing the sword of light away into the dust.

'No!' he heard Jesse yell, swooping above the mob, desperately trying to snatch him away.

But it was too late.

The Doers descended on the Dragon Hunter. He disappeared beneath a blur of hands and fangs. The Doers howled victoriously, like hounds baying for more blood. They drank their fill.

*

'Break the spell, awaken to me,' the Dragon Hunter heard the voice say. Warm white light filled his mind, caressed it, healed it. The illusion of his sacrifice to the Doers faded like a bad nightmare. The face inside the hood came rushing into view.

'How can this be?' the Dragon Hunter said, rubbing his bleary eyes.

The cloaked and hooded figure emerged from behind the altar.

'We need to hurry. Explanations later. You were deep inside the bat's mind charm. I found it difficult to break the magic. But it is done now. For the moment, you are safe.'

'Thank you. It's good to have you back.'

'I wish I could say it's good to be back, but we are surrounded by dark evil forces and more are coming.'

'The Riders?'

'Most definitely. But there are more than them. The Driths are close – Dendrith, Gwendrith, Jagdrith and Kildrith. And the Skaardrithadon has sent his own foul creations, moulded from his cloud of darkness and brought to life by portions of his own glow. He calls these brutal killers – the Brood.'

'How do we get out of this mess?'

'Good question. I wish I knew the answer.'

The echoing silence of the church engulfed the

Dragon Hunter momentarily. The musty smell of ancient wood and dampness entered his nostrils. He shuddered. He was not certain whether from cold or fear. He felt uncomfortable in this place. There were too many dark shadows, too many stained-glass vampire saints peering down, too many cold stone statues that threatened to come to life. Irrational fears assailed his usually fearless logical mind for a moment or two. Then he caught hold of himself, got a grip of his mind and the games it played. The giant bat was trying to re-enter his mind. He shut it out.

'So what next?' he said at last. His voice echoed in the darkness.

'Once we have gathered Jesse and the rest together, we will continue the journey across the desert to find and release Perigold.'

'Do you know where the Skaardrithadon is?'

'Yes,' Zarlan-Jagr said, lowering his head to reveal his shining spirit face. 'Follow me.'

The Dragon Hunter's jaw dropped in astonishment. The wizard, Zarlan-Jagr, was a ghost.

Seven

Spells and Sand

Jesse shook her head again and stared in disbelief at the shining wizard, Zarlan-Jagr. They were sitting around a sparking campfire miles away from the ruined village and temple. They had flown as close to the ground as they could, over the never-ending orange sheen of a vast desert. Eventually, as the ruby sun dipped behind the distant mountains, they had landed at a tiny oasis. The oasis was encircled by succulent palm trees and coarse grasses. It was not wise to travel across the open dark desert. Night time was prime time for the vampire creatures. So, here they were, huddled around a camp fire which they had made from dry sticks and palm leaves. The moon's silver reflection was mirrored in the oasis's still waters. Deep shadows shifted across the sand, given life by the gently swaying palm trees.

'Tell the story again,' Jake said excitedly. 'It's unreal.'

'You need sleep, Jake,' Zarlan-Jagr smiled and pulled on his hood. His teeth flashed snowy white, and like the rest of his face were strangely transparent one moment and seemingly solid the next. 'And you, too, Jesse. Indeed, all of you should rest. We have another day of draining travel ahead of us.'

'But the story? Tell us the bit where Zundrith killed you. That was awesome,' Jake said, his eyes glittering like the stars above them in the flickering fire light.

'Please, tell it again.'

'Yes, pleasing.' Iggywig was polishing off the last of the magic food Zarlan-Jagr had conjured from his mind – egg custards, chops and a particular desert favourite of his, grass platter. 'Tis a magnificent tale of wizardry and witchery!'

Zarlan-Jagr told the story of his part in the Battle for Caldazar. They howled with laughter at Zundrith's brother, turning into a child again. They were open-mouthed at Zarlan-Jagr's transition from ordinary wizard to a transcended wizard-spirit who now had the power to live in many dimensions of existence all at the same time.

'That was wonderful, wizard,' the Dragon Hunter said from his watch-out position amongst the palm trees. Kumo Diaz was guarding the opposite side of the oasis, restlessly scanning east and south. 'You are full of honour, a hero. It is good to have you back with us again.'

'It is good to be back, but you should not be listening,' Zarlan-Jagr said. 'Be watchful, my friend. The dark is crammed with danger.'

The Dragon Hunter nodded and surveyed the north west. He could just see the faint glimmer of the ruined village in the distance.

'How long has it been since the Battle for Caldazar?' Jesse asked. She was curious to know how long they had been travelling in the Skaardrithadon's cloud.

'Almost three days.'

'Three days?' Jesse's mind swirled. 'Are you sure?'

'Yes.'

'Tis no wonder that Iggywig's rumblings be a-growing like an exploding volcano in his tummy.'

Jake laughed. 'Yes! I had three days of solid sleep. How cool is that?'

Jesse shook her head. 'You're sad, Jake.'

'Thank you,' Jake mocked. 'So kind.'

Jesse's mind was brimming with questions for the spirit-wizard. 'So how is it possible for you to be with us *and* be in other places at the same time?' she asked.

'I have no idea,' Zarlan-Jagr said. 'But it is a reality.'

'What are you doing? Where are you? What's-'

'One question at a time, Jesse, please,' the wizard spirit said. 'It's very complicated, and a little odd to be in so many places all at once. I'm sleeping in the mayor's exquisite guest bedroom in Alisbad in the Kingdom of Troth. The mayor has been most kind. One of my many selves has to rest sometimes.'

Jesse nodded her understanding.

'How is Alisbad?' the Dragon Hunter said from his watch-out post.

'Alisbad is relaxed and peaceful. The Calm made sure of that. But, please, pay attention to your watch.'

'And Kayblade? Have you spoken to the Master Storyteller lately?' Jesse asked, shuddering at the memory of her story telling ordeal.

'No, I have not spoken with him. But he is still telling his stories. People come from far and near to hear them. Nothing has changed there.'

'And Dendrith's castle?' Kumo Diaz spoke at last from the other side of the oasis. 'Has that been rebuilt?'

'Yes, but the witch has never returned. The Rumble remade it, fashioned it into a glorious building. Ulek and his family of giants have taken vacant possession of the new castle. They've grown bored with Dragon Cove and have decided to turn Dendrith's castle into a tourist attraction. They've hired a few Spriggans to haunt the dungeons to give it an authentic feel.'

Jesse laughed and then frowned as her mind drifted to her mother. 'Are you living in the human world, too?'

'One of my selves is located in the human world. I keep an eye on things, lurk about Chestnut Lane disguised as a road sweeper.'

'You're kidding?'

'No. It sounds ridiculous, doesn't it? But because your family are on many dark fairies' hit lists, they need around-the-clock protection. So far there have been no incidents. Your mum and dad are fine, Jesse. They send their love.'

Jesse swallowed back tears and stared into the flickering flames. For a moment she longed for her old life – school, hanging out with friends, looking after Bonnie. And then the Scratchits had come along and everything had changed. Surely you don't want to go back to that life of slavery? She did not. Never. But things were back to the way they used to be now. Mum and Dad were together again, and their home was the way it used to be before the Scratchits arrived and ruined everything. She yearned for those old times, those quiet peaceful times. Lazy summer days of sunshine and early morning birdsong. During the school summer holiday she was up with the lark, wandering the country lanes, strolling through shining fields of wheat. Those days seemed still, calm, not a breath of wind. Perfect. Not anymore though. Since her arrival in the Fairy Kingdoms, her life had been a mad race against dark forces out to rob her of one thing or another. She sighed heavily and looked up from the flames.

'You have grown beyond your human life, Jesse,' Zarlan-Jagr said, as if reading her thoughts. 'You are a soothsayer, fairy shape-shifter and much more. Now that the obsidian Seeing-Stone has merged with you, your life has moved on, changed.'

'Yes, I know,' she said, shaking her thoughts away. She smiled thinly. 'Keep an eye on mum and dad, will you? I worry about them.'

'Of course I will.'

There was a moment of silence, each of them reflective – staring into the flames. The dark desert was eerily silent. Small animal sounds from miles away carried across the desert – snuffles, a lone howl, a growl. A blazing palm leaf spat a spark out of the fire.

Jesse jumped, Jake laughed.

'How many places can you live in at the same time?' Jake said, his young unbroken voice thick with admiration.

'Too many.'

'Five? Ten?'

'More.'

'More?' Jake's voice rose like a siren. 'How many more?'

'As I said – too many.'

'What do you mean?' Jesse said.

'With this power comes great responsibility.'

'The Code of the Union of Thirteen, you mean?'

Zarlan-Jagr glanced across the flames at Trondian-Yor, who had sat impassively chewing a tip of vampire-grass. He enjoyed the bitter-sweetness. The old spirit-wizard's eyes asked many questions.

Trondian-Yor felt him probe his mind, seek the extent of information he had given up to Jesse regarding the Union and then he let go, relaxed, satisfied. She knew a little, but not enough to put any of them in danger. Secrets, knowledge, magic. Ancient secrets, ancient knowledge, ancient magic. She was not ready for it – yet. Perhaps she never would be ready. Perhaps she would come to join their ranks, create a new Union? Perhaps not. There were many possibilities. Her future was not clear. It was misty, a cloud of possibilities.

'The Union of Thirteen's Code has little meaning unless *all* its members follow it,' Zarlan-Jagr said. 'And yes, my responsibilities are far greater as a transcended member. But that is not a concern for anyone here. Both Trondian-Yor and I will keep watch. Rest now – sleep.'

Zarlan-Jagr wriggled the fingers of his ringless hand. They glittered. A thin blue mist poured from them, washing gently over the companions. They all slept deeply throughout the night, while Zarlan-Jagr talked with Trondian-Yor about the dreadful capture of Perigold, and the abduction of the remaining members of the Union of Thirteen.

*

'The Skaardrithadon has changed them all into his vampire slaves,' Zarlan-Jagr said.

Dusky grey moonlight bathed them, casting long narrow shadows, except where Zarlan-Jagr sat, a ghost clad in robes. His insubstantial body was shadowless.

'All of the sleepers?' Trondian-Yor said, a quiver splitting his voice.

'Yes – he has them all.'

'What happened to May Demigould?'

'Her body was the only one left in the chamber at Talonscar.'

'She still walks in spirit with the Ascended Ones of Old?'

'Yes. She is in good company – Elriad's wonders refresh her, teach her the Hidden Wisdom.'

Trondian-Yor sighed with relief. 'At least this dark news has some light.'

'Some, but not much.'

'And Laike du Puttchen? He transcended years ago – just like you – struck down in battle, a walker of many worlds all at once.'

'I have not been able to find Laike du Puttchen. Unfortunately for us.'

'So the Union of Thirteen is just two?'

'Yes – me and you.'

Trondian-Yor gazed at the sleeping companions and shook his head. 'These are brave folk. But they are no match for the magic of the eight Union members under the Skaardrithadon's control. He will surely use all of the power they possess against us.'

'No doubt. But what choice do we have? We must track down the Skaardrithadon, let Jesse and Jake unleash the Curse of Caldazar, and pray that the vampire blood cells have not totally taken over the eight.'

'I agree. We still have a little time on our side.'

'Good – then at first light we break camp and head for the Skaardrithadon's lair at the foot of the Dead End Mountains.'

Trondian-Yor paused for a second. He looked

toward the dark distant silhouette of the mountains. He shook his head, puzzled. 'We are no closer now than we've ever been.'

Zarlan-Jagr raised an eyebrow.

'The mountains keep moving,' Trondian-Yor said.

'No, my young wizard friend. You are closer than you believe. You are almost there. It's an illusion, a Vampire Lord's mind trick. Look.'

Some unseen wave of energy rippled through his mind as if a stone had been tossed into a calm lake. Trondian-Yor felt the wizard's counter charm sweep through him, cleansing. He squinted to see the imposing silhouette of the Dead End Mountains. They were no more than ten miles away. Perhaps less.

'They're enormous,' he said, craning his neck to make out the dark jagged profile of the several mountain peaks. 'Do you know the way to the Skaardrithadon's lair?'

'Yes. But it is not an easy journey. I only hope that the Ancient Wizard of Elriad's prophesy is worthy.'

'Which prophesy is that, may I ask?'

The spirit-wizard did not answer. Trondian-Yor did not ask again.

*

At first light, they broke camp and buried the grey ash and embers of the fire beneath the sand. Like the desert behind them, the one before them was vast, white-orange, blinding. Great dunes rose like mini mountains a few miles ahead. There was no track or road, and the sand beneath their feet was soft and draining in places and a baked hardpan in others.

'It's like walking under water,' Jesse said struggling to lift her legs as she climbed up a dune.

'Stop complaining,' the Dragon Hunter snapped. He had been grumpy all morning, since Zarlan-Jagr had advised him to bury most of his armour beneath the oasis sands. The wizard had warned him about the harsh zapping desert and hot unrelenting sun. After a full five minutes of protesting, the Dragon Hunter had reluctantly buried the armour when he'd been told that he would "cook inside the metal like a turkey in an oven turned up to full power."

'I'm not complaining. I'm just saying.'

'It's hot and I'm tired,' Jake said, sipping from a hide water-bag Zarlan-Jagr had given him back at the oasis. 'Can we rest a minute?'

Iggywig wiped sweat from his forehead with the back of his hand. 'Tis a fine idea, kind Jake.'

'It's been hours,' Jake groaned. 'I need a rest.'

'We've been walking just over twenty minutes,' Zarlan-Jagr said. 'We agreed to rest every hour for five minutes.'

'But I'm hot and tired. I want to rest now.'

'We are all tired and hot,' Trondian-Yor said. 'Focus on something other than the heat and your tiredness, Jake.'

'I can't.'

'Then stop moaning,' the Dragon Hunter said. 'You are depressing me.'

'Why do we have to walk?' Jake said, licking his parched lips.

'You know why.' Jesse reached the top of the dune and offered her hand to Jake, who was slipping and sliding in the sand beneath her. 'Zarlan-Jagr has already explained.'

'But it makes no sense. You should use magic. Iggywig and Trondian-Yor both fly, you and Cyren fly too. Zarlan-Jagr could use his magic to fly. But no! We take the torture option. Ridiculous. Why can't we take to the air and fly?'

'Too risky, young Jake,' Zarlan-Jagr said, pushing him from behind the top of the dune. 'Now please stop talking. You are wasting your energy.'

'Yes, stop moaning,' the Dragon Hunter echoed. 'And give me a hand up this damn dune!'

Jesse watched Jake and Zarlan-Jagr haul the Dragon Hunter up. Iggywig was next, followed by Kumo Diaz, and Trondian-Yor. Cyren, despite his great size, seemed made for desert travel. He clambered over the dune with relative ease and slid down the other side. His huge feet acted like paddles.

'Why can't you use magic? We'd be at the mountains in minutes,' Jake moaned again, dropping to his knees in protest.

'It's too dangerous,' Zarlan-Jagr said patiently. 'The scent of our magic would be picked up on the breeze very quickly. The Skaardrithadon would pinpoint our position. He probably has a good idea where we are from the magic already used. But I doubt he knows where we are exactly. So now we stop using magic until the time is right to use it again. We also need to surprise him, try to catch him off guard. So, chin up, Jake. Not far now. We are close to his lair.'

'So get up and get on with it,' the Dragon Hunter said, hauling Jake to his feet. 'Otherwise I will hold your hand like a baby every step of the way.'

Jake got up slowly and trudged through the sand without a word. Jesse smirked. Kumo Diaz saw Jesse smirk and smiled at her, remaining close. Each step was one step nearer to his dream, one step nearer to her nightmare.

Eight

Trance

'Do you see them yet?' Kildrith said. 'My arms are aching. I need a rest.'

'Stop your whining, warlock,' Gwendrith said. 'Can't you see my sister is deep in communication with the Skaardrithadon?'

The Driths were gathered around the oasis where Jesse and her companions had rested the night before. Dendrith was crouched at the water's edge, peering trance-like into the blue cool liquid. Dazzling sunlight sparkled at its edge. The palm leaves and vampire grass rustled in the intermittent breeze. The cruel force of the sun's heat burned the lily white skin of their hands.

'I'm drying like a prune, sister,' Gwendrith said, slipping the cuffs of her cloak back over her hands. 'This blasted heat is sucking every drop of moisture from my skin.'

'How can it be? You are a ghost.'

'So what? I'm sensitive. I hate the sunlight.'

'Who's whinging now?' Kildrith said, still clutching the stiff owl and Jagdrith in his arms.

'Who's afraid of getting a tan?'

'Shut your stinking warlock trap.' Gwendrith said, glaring at him.

'Or what?'

'Or I'll shut it once and for all.'

Kildrith's laugh was hollow and short. 'I'm waiting,' he said. 'When is this wonderful gob-shutting event going to happen? Tomorrow? Next week? Next year? Or do you need a little more time to lcarn a spell or practice your pathetic magic on a toad or a frog?'

'I'm warning you for the last time, warlock. Keep it shut or I'll-'

'Yes!' Dendrith yelled gleefully. 'I see them. I see them!'

'Where are they?' Gwendrith said, hurrying to her sister's side and peering into the water. 'Where?'

'Close – just a few miles east. They are just struggling up a dune. How pathetic they look on foot.'

'Do you see Jameson?' Kildrith said.

'Yes. I see them all.'

'Let's take them now,' Gwendrith said. 'Surprise them. Kill them. Take revenge!'

'No,' Dendrith said, rising and dusting away the sand from her cloak. She examined her talons, flicked dirt from them with a shiny metal nail-file she produced from thin air. 'Not yet. The New Master of Darkness will send a sign, a vision, something. This is his domain, the Naargapire. It is best to do things his way. We will continue to follow at a safe distance.'

'But they are so close,' Gwendrith said. 'We could have the job over and done out here in the desert. They are virtually defenceless in the open.'

'I hate to admit it,' Kildrith said, 'but she's right.

Why wait?'

'Because the Skaardrithadon says wait,' Dendrith said. 'Put down my daughter and her owl very carefully.'

'Thank you,' Kildrith said, lowering them and rubbing his aching arms. 'That was most painful.'

'Good,' Dendrith said. She pushed Kildrith aside. 'Now out of my way. It's time to release them, to warm them up. What better place than this desert?'

Gwendrith cackled. 'Oh, good – a spell! Can I help, dearest sister?'

'Yes,' Dendrith said. Of course you can, dear dear sister of mine.'

'How?'

'Stand back and keep your trap shut.'

Kildrith smirked, Gwendrith did not.

'What kind of magic, dearest sister?' Gwendrith said excitedly. 'What incantation or spell will you perform?'

'Place them side by side, back to back,' Dendrith ordered Kildrith. 'Dig two little holes and stand them in them. Make sure they are secure. Be certain they won't fall over. Yes, dig right now. That would be good.'

Kildrith reluctantly moved Jagdrith first, scooping out a small hole in the sand like a turtle preparing to lay its eggs. I'd love to smash them all like eggs – damn witches, he thought. He stood Jagdrith's petrified body in the hole and then filled it with sand. She seemed sturdy enough.

'Perhaps, dearest sister,' Gwendrith said, 'the warlock could build us a few sandcastles. He seems to be enjoying his game in the sand!'

'You are so funny, sister,' Dendrith said, not smiling. 'You make me want to puke.'

'Oh, thank you, sister dear, that's the kindest

thing you've said today. Can I puke too?'

The warlock dug the second hole without looking up at them.

'If you like,' Dendrith said, shrugging.

'Thank you, sister. I'll puke on the warlock.'

Dendrith's ghost lips twisted into a delighted smile. 'Good idea, dear sister. But why waste good sick on a stinking rat like him?'

They howled, cackled wildly.

Kildrith ignored them, placing the owl in another hole next to Jagdrith. He back filled it so that the owl wouldn't topple over. He brushed his hands on his cloak and wandered off into a small stand of palm trees. He was sick of them and sick of the blasted heat of the sun. He sheltered in the shade, watching them impassively. He crouched down, back leaning against a tree trunk.

'Oh, sister, tell me what kind of trickery and magic you'll perform to release our Sister in Suffering and her owl eyes?'

Dendrith pushed by Gwendrith, her face darkening with the concentration of incantation. She spat green mucus into her taloned hands and rubbed them together. In seconds a small green ball of spit had formed, as if made from rubber. She tossed it into the oasis, turning the clear blue life-giving water into a foul undrinkable green pool of slime.

'Brullvargcha! Brullvargchi!'

She chanted the two Ancient Witch words over and over. The palm trees swayed and bent with the violent winds of the spell. Branches and tree trunks moaned as they bowed. Kildrith clung to his hat, cursing her. He narrowed his eyes to slits as the sand thrashed about his ruined face. He covered his mouth and nose with a dirty white handkerchief he'd conjured from his sleeve. The palm trees creaked alarmingly, bent over like old men. The sand-choked wind continued to sting and bite. Vampire grass was flattened at the edge of the oasis. A sand storm whipped up about them, eddying around Jagdrith and her owl until they became a blur within the vortex of sand.

'Return to me! Release the spell!' Dendrith raged, her voice tiny amongst the howling sand storm.

'Now! Be gone!'

The storm stopped, sand dropped, trees stilled, Kildrith dusted himself down. The still air smelled dry and hot.

'Impressive, sister dear,' Gwendrith said. 'But your spell didn't work.'

Dendrith glided over to Jagdrith, picked her daughter up like a stiff porcelain doll, and threw her into the oasis. There was a muffled spatter, like a contestant being tossed into a pool of gunk on a wacky TV games show. Jagdrith sank slowly beneath the green goo. Dendrith grabbed the owl by the scruff of its neck and threw it into the slime, too. It hit the thick surface with a horrid splat, and sank slowly without trace.

'Brullvargcha!   Brullvargchi!   Brullvargchu! Brullvargcho!

The spell had changed, multiplied. The reeking green oasis did not stir. A minute passed.

'Brullvargcha!   Brullvargchi!   Brullvargchu! Brullvargcho!

Three vampire parrots dropped dead out of a nearby palm tree and hit Kildrith on the head.

'What the!' the warlock yelled, jumping to his feet, waving away red, blue and yellow feathers.

Gwendrith laughed.

Dendrith scowled and continued to chant the foul

witch words again and again. Over and over. In a rhythmic pulse that even sent shivers of anxiety down the unfeeling Kildrith's spine. He moved away from the palm trees, muttering something unpleasant, and stood in the sunlight.

Gwendrith scanned the treetops, eager for more parrots.

Nothing – not in the slime of the oasis or in the tree tops.

Two minutes passed.

'How long can she go without air?' Gwendrith said.

'Not too long, I hope,' Kildrith said.

'What did you say?'

'I said we may need a long rope.' Kildrith couldn't hide a twisted smile. 'To pull them out, if the spell fails.'

'My sister's spell will not fail.'

'We shall see,' Kildrith said, cursing the sun.

Three minutes passed.

Dendrith did not miss a beat of her incantation. She chanted louder than before. The rhythm rose and fell in volume. Wild things howled somewhere out in the desert.

Five minutes passed.

'Perhaps I should conjure a rope,' Kildrith said. 'Pull them out before they drown.'

Gwendrith looked at her sister, seeking reassurance. She found none. Perhaps the warlock was right? She glanced back anxiously at him.

Kildrith raised his eyebrows, forlornly.

'Sister?' Gwendrith sounded uneasy. 'Do we need a rope?'

Dendrith chanted on, slipping into a wide-eyed trance. If she heard her sister, she chose to ignore her. But in truth she was leaving this world, drifting quickly into the twilight world of spells and magic. Her hands were trembling. Dark things slipped in and out of her mouth. Her cloak rippled at the hem from its own breeze. Grains of sand began to swirl around her in a circular motion. Anti-clockwise.

Ten minutes went by. The vortex of sand was so thick now that the lower half of Dendrith's body could not be seen.

'This is pointless,' Kildrith said, gliding back under the shade of the palm trees. He rearranged his hat, wiping his sweaty brow with the back of his ape-like hand. 'They're dead.'

'Sister?'

On and on went the chanting. Up and up rose the eddying sand until the witch was completely engulfed. Her cloak flapped about her wildly. Her hair was a billowing, tangled mess. The only sound now was the coarse swishing of sand and cloak.

Gwendrith licked her lips fretfully. Kildrith whistled tunelessly, gazing, bored, in to the canopy above him. He hated the suspense of the witch's magic. It went on and on and on. He was a flash, bang, wallop warlock. His style was simple: a single bolt of sizzling lightning usually solved disputes and problems quickly.

Dendrith stopped chanting. The vortex of sand stopped swirling, dropping in a circular mound around her. She bent down and grabbed a handful of hot sand. She watched in silence as it trickled from her fingers.

'Sand and time,' she whispered strangely. 'Sand runs, but time stands still for my daughter.'

Gwendrith looked at her, dumbfounded.

Dendrith leapt up and her dark cloak and hair billowed wildly. 'Now it reverses for her, sister.'

'What do you mean?' Gwendrith said.

88

'She lives again.'

The oasis rippled on the surface. Small bubbles of slime popped and spluttered. Air beneath the goo was escaping. Then suddenly a mighty surge of energy shot both the owl and Jagdrith out of the oasis. They hit the sand with a thump. A great wad of green slime hit Kildrith, knocking his hat off, and covering his head and shoulders. He swore loudly.

'Return to us, daughter,' Dendrith said.

Jagdrith stood up on wobbly legs, and wiped the slime from her eyes.

'Yes, that's it. Return.'

Jagdrith opened her eyes. 'I can see again!'

Dendrith nodded satisfyingly. 'Yes, you can see again, daughter.'

'Impressive witchery, sister,' Gwendrith said. She applauded. 'Very dramatic. Brilliant.'

Kildrith scowled, wiping slime from his head.

Nine

Dead End Mountains

The desert sun beat down on them as they trudged across the great sea of sand. There was no let up in the burning, blistering rays. Jesse had pulled up the collar of her shirt to protect her neck, but the top of her head was sore. No doubt it had been burnt. The first place she always burned when exposed to too much sun was the thin line of flesh between her parting. The second was the length of her nose. It was also sore and tender. She tried to ignore the pain, but it was hard. She longed for Zarlan-Jagr to use his magic. He could have conjured a baseball cap to shield her from the sun. But he'd explained that is was not wise to use magic in the Naargapire any longer. Magic carried scents and they would soon be discovered. Best to walk. Yes, best to resist the urge to conjure, until it was the last course of action. No, until it was the *only* way to get them closer to Perigold.

They travelled for hours, crawling up sand hills as high as three story houses. They crossed belts of dunes, and clambered over hard-edged sandstone mounds, baked solid by the fierce sunlight. For several miles, the desert became hardpan – flat, concrete-like, cracked. There was no vegetation at all. The hardpan was barren. Out here, exposed to the harsh elements, the sun's rays were sapping them. Their pace had slowed dramatically the further they travelled until it was a huge effort to move one foot in front of the other. They drank more water than they should have, but it was incredibly hot. The heat shimmered just above the hardpan in the distance, and within that shimmering heat they saw strange things. Illusion or real, they were not sure. Tall dark creatures appeared and disappeared. Palm trees stood high one moment, then they vanished the next.

One time, Jake was convinced he'd seen an oasis brimming with water out there in the heat shimmer, but they never reached it. It was a mirage, nothing more than a trick of the desert. Jesse was wiping sweat from her stinging eyes when Jake let out another cry of delight. This time what he'd spotted was not a mirage. The vast open hardpan had an end in sight. High dunes stood out in the distance. Tiny now but the closer they walked, the larger they became. This was not an illusion. Perhaps they would find water beyond them. Hope filled their hearts and their pace quickened. They walked on and on, gasping, sweating, swaying on wobbly exhausted legs. Almost two hours later they reached the dunes, collapsed to their hands and knees, as if praying in religious ecstasy, crawled up them, and stood gazing down from the top.

They saw an awful sight. No, this was not what they wanted to see. They wanted cool clear water, an oasis where they could rest beneath the shade of palm trees. This was not it.

'What is it?' Jesse said, her mouth hot and dry. It hurt to talk.

'Vampire dead,' Zarlan-Jagr said. 'Best not go down there. We'll walk around the rim.'

Jesse was shocked by the size of the huge hollow in the sand. It was a massive bowl, stretching hundreds of yards ahead of them.

'Cool,' Jake said, cheering up instantly. 'Skulls and bones.'

'You're sick,' Jesse said. 'There's nothing cool about thousands of dead creatures.'

'Don't see any flesh or blood,' Jake said, smiling with gruesome delight. 'Too rotten for that – just skulls and bones.'

'Sick.'

'Excellent. The kid's at school would be so jealous. How many skulls do you think are down there?'

'Too many,' Jesse said, following Zarlan-Jagr along the edge of the bowl. The rest followed, slowly.

'What's this place called?' Jake said.

Iggywig and Trondian-Yor shrugged. Kumo Diaz and the Dragon Hunter shook their heads.

'I think it's Restless Skull Hollow,' Trondian-Yor said.

'Restless skull what?' Jake said.

'Hollow – like hole, something empty,' Trondian-Yor added.

'Like your head, Jake,' Jesse said, a sparkle in her eyes.

'Funny,' he said, not laughing.

Iggywig smirked.

Jake stopped, mesmerised by the gleaming white vampire skulls and the bleached white sand everywhere inside the crater. He squinted and held up a red sunburned hand to his eyes to shield them from the glare.

'Why's the sand orange up here and white down there?' Jake said.

Iggywig was the last to trudge by him.

'Tis bonemeal, kind Jake.'

'What?'

'Be a-pardon, not what.' Iggywig's kaleidoscope eyes twirled playfully. 'And be not sand all whiting and powdering, but bone.'

'Bone?'

'Bones made into bone dust by the weather,' Trondian-Yor said. 'Crushed bone.'

'Cool – crushed bone. Who crushed it?'

'Time,' Zarlan-Jagr said, not glancing over his shoulder but watching carefully the way forward. The sand here around the rim was soft. 'Now please keep up. The dead still see and hear.'

'Cool,' Jake said, smiling, and he trudged after them with new life in his stride. 'Perhaps I'll get to talk to the dead.'

They ignored his childish glee.

He didn't see the rippling sand behind him, as if an invisible snake was sliding quickly in his direction.

*

Jesse struggled through the sand around the rim of the titanic hollow. Ahead the mountains loomed with deceptive clarity. Zarlan-Jagr was stepping out in front, and the rest of them were trailed behind, gazing down at the grains of never-ending orange. Cyren brought up the rear now, struggling to keep up now that they were travelling on sinking soft sand. They were about half way around Restless Skull Hollow, and the sun's unrelenting rays were getting hotter and hotter.

'Why can't we go down there and walk?' Jake

93

said. 'It would be so much easier, a lot quicker.'

'You can't walk across the bones and skulls of the dead,' Jesse snapped.

'But what harm will it do?' Jake quickened his pace and sidled up to Jesse. He pulled a goofy face. 'They're dead. They won't feel a thing.'

Jesse stared at Jake. Before she entered the Fairy Kingdoms, back when they were just ordinary kids hanging out in an ordinary school playground, she used to laugh at Jake's goofy face. He would pull it just before a joke. His jokes were usually stupid and infantile, but she liked him; not his jokes. He was a laugh. Today, though, she couldn't laugh. Everything here at Restless Skull Hollow was too serious, too sad.

The hardpan had been awful, a draining, exhausting experience. And now they were in trouble again. There were also the nagging thoughts of her magic entering her mind. Out here, in the desert, thought had replaced conversation. Yes, plenty of time to think. Her life had been transformed. She had many thoughts swirling around inside that she couldn't sort out. The thought of them made her feel giddy. The power of her new magic had impressed her, but now she worried about it. How had the obsidian Seeing-Stone fused to her hand? Why hadn't she felt pain? How had it been possible to shoot sparks and storm from her palm back at the Innermost Sanctum and not feel any pain whatsoever? What was going on? Her mind drew a blank. She didn't know, but refocused on Jake again. His goofy face just wasn't right – wrong time and place, Jake, she thought. Wrong time, wrong place.

'Grow up, Jake,' she said.

'I would, but it's just not possible at the moment.

I'm just a kid.'

And there was the problem. Jesse felt more than a child now. Changes had happened inside her mind and body which made her feel different. She felt alien. She was at odds with the rest of them, and herself. That was the worst of it. She knew she had changed, had become bossy and over-bearing, but she didn't know how to stop. She wasn't sure she *wanted* to stop. It was as if she'd become another person. It was hard to come to terms with, and at that moment impossible for her to understand fully. But she would try to understand her new self as best she could. It was hard, but she would try.

They trudged on in silence around the rim. They could see some way off the stepped incline of the desert, rising into foothills and barren grey slopes. The bedrock erupted like solid volcanoes of puss on the earth's sallow skin. Higher, the land formed a plateau of trees, dense and green and lush. Higher still, a thick white layer of cloud clung to the snow-capped peaks.

'The mountains are beautiful,' Jesse said to no-one in particular.

'Whatever,' Jake said.

Zarlan-Jagr stopped and offered the children his water bag. 'The Dead End Mountains are harsh and dangerous, populated by clans of vampires. But there is no denying it – they are beautiful in their own way.'

'How many vampires?' Jesse took a sip of water. There wasn't much left. She gently wiped her tender mouth with her fingertips and handed the water bag to Jake.

'It's hard to say exactly. But I will try to find out. Wait a moment please.'

Zarlan-Jagr paused, switched from one life to

another. In a way it was like switching from one TV channel to another. The desert faded as he focused on the mountains. He was perched in a tree on the lush slopes above them. His magpie-self watched the vampire creatures below. Dozens flitted in and out of the Skaardrithadon's lair. Hundreds of giant bats were roosting just inside the entrance. Their red eyes were dull and unblinking.

He flew up and over the lower narrow paths, spotting groups of Doers, who were guarding the route to the lair. Below he saw no life on the sloped incline, but amongst the foothills thousands of misty mottled creatures were gathered in four large platoons. Other vampire creatures skulked in the undergrowth, birds, insects, animals. It did not look promising. The odds against them were most unfavourable.

Zarlan-Jagr's return to the desert was swift and effortless, like switching from one memory to another. He slipped into his spirit-wizard self like a snake into water. Smooth, noiseless, easy.

'The Skaardrithadon is well-protected,' he said. 'We will not be able to sneak through.'

'Why not?' Jesse said.

'There are too many against us. When we reach the foothills we'll show ourselves, use all the magic we possess.'

'Good. At last we fight. How many are there?' the Dragon Hunter said.

'Several thousand.'

'Several thousand? Jake's voice jumped an octave. He gulped.

The spirit-wizard nodded.

Jesse put her arm around Jake's shoulder. He was trembling.

'We could go around them,' Kumo Diaz said.

96

'What would be the point of that?' the Dragon Hunter said tersely. 'Perigold is in the Skaardrithadon's lair. Going around the mountains would take us away from him, not closer to him.'

Jesse stared at Kumo Diaz. It was a strange thing to say.

'Yes, you are right,' Kumo Diaz conceded. 'That was a stupid idea. I'm sorry.'

The Dragon Hunter grunted something obscene and strode away. His hand rested on the hilt of his sword, fingers twitching, staring ahead at the foothills.

Jesse felt sorry for the tracker and offered him a consolatory look.

Kumo Diaz shrugged, pretending to be embarrassed. Inside, he was glowing. He was a step closer to her. She felt sorry for him. He definitely had her hooked now, and was reeling her in, slowly but surely like a huge fish.

'Then we fight,' the Dragon Hunter said, gripping the hilt and scanning the mountainside with his golden binocular eyes.

'You're mad,' Jake said. 'Thousands? You seriously think we stand a chance against thousands?'

'What is the alternative?'

Jake shrugged his shoulders. He glanced down at the bleached bones of the vampire dead. Dark eye sockets peered at him. 'Turn back.'

'What?' Jesse withdrew her arm from his shoulder. 'Jake?'

'Never,' the Dragon Hunter said in a low voice. 'I owe Perigold my life.'

'But it's stupid,' Jake said. He was shaking more than ever, despite the heat. 'Look at us? We don't stand a chance.'

'I can't turn back, Jake,' Jesse said. She couldn't believe he'd said what he'd said. Even though his logic was spot on, his lack of loyalty was non-existent. 'I just can't.'

'It's simple,' Jake said. He motioned with a sweeping hand behind him. 'Look. We just turn around and walk back the way we came.'

Jesse glanced toward the oasis. If only time could be turned back, she thought. So that none of this had happened. She and Jake would still be growing up together, going to school at St. Wormdirt's Primary, playing up at the field after school. Life was so simple then. But not anymore. Life had always been a list of choices. Every moment. No matter how hard. No matter how impossible. And besides, she told herself, she was different now – the Magiceye, the Obsidian Container, the Seeing-Stone. Yes, these things were incredible, impossible to a narrow mind, but they were indisputable. There was no going back. So many discoveries, so many gifts. She would have to use them, to help save Perigold. Maybe then they would go back. But now? No, not now. She had come too far. 'No,' she said at last. 'I will not turn back. I will not walk away.'

'But this is madness,' Jake said. 'You have magic powers, Jesse.' He pointed to the others. 'He is a dragon killer, and they are wizards, even Iggywig has magic. What chance do I stand in battle?'

'Very little,' said Kumo Diaz, feeding the child's fear. 'Both you and I seem to be at a disadvantage here.'

'Yes,' said Jake. 'We are. But you're an adult. You're a tracker, too. You are much stronger than I am. You're smarter, too. And I bet you know how to fight, don't you?'

Kumo Diaz nodded. 'Yes, Jake. You are right. I'm

stronger than you, and I've had to fight for my life a few times out in the wilderness.'

'So you see my point?'

'Yes,' said Zarlan-Jagr, joining them. 'We all see your point, Jake. You are scared. You are just an ordinary human child, but you are more than that.'

'What do you mean?'

'You are Jesse's friend. And without you, if you turn back now, our mission will fail.'

'The Curse of Caldazar, you mean?'

'Yes, we need you and Jesse to chant the curse together. Only then will the Skaardrithadon be sent back to his prison in the Innermost Sanctum. We can't do it without you.'

'We need you, Jake,' Jesse said. 'Perigold needs you. I need you.'

Jake blushed. Hearing those words made him feel good inside, wanted. 'All right,' he said at last. 'I won't turn back. But it's complete madness. You know that don't you? We are out-numbered badly. It's an impossible thing we have to do.'

'Yes, Jake,' Zarlan-Jagr said. 'It will not be easy, but the very future of the Union of Thirteen depends upon our success.'

Jake shrugged. 'I don't care about your Union.'

'I know,' he said softly. His ghost face shimmered. 'But one day you will – you will care very much.'

Jake looked at the spirit-wizard as if he was hopelessly mad.

*

Jesse trudged further around the never-ending rim, silent and brooding. It really was a very long way. Deceptively so. Much further than she'd originally thought. Nowhere near as far as the trek across the hardpan, but draining in the soft sand. The heat was unbearable, too, and she felt it sapping her strength very quickly. She needed a rest, even though they had only walked for fifteen minutes. Her mouth was awfully dry and her face was dripping with sweat. It ran down her temples and into her eyes. It stung. Her lips were tender, painful, swollen. Her tongue was so dry it kept sticking to the roof of her mouth. She wanted to take little sips of water to moisten it, but if she drank then Jake would want to as well. Their small supply would soon be gone. She had to stop thinking about water and her uncomfortable condition. She must concentrate on their goal – Perigold was closer now than he'd ever been.

A yelp made her jump.

She looked back at Jake, who had been walking behind her, but had now stopped. He yelped again. Something stirred beneath Jake's feet. He jumped. Jesse stepped back. The Dragon Hunter unsheathed his glowing sword. Little puffs of fine sand wafted up. Then the movement beneath them stopped.

'What was that?' Jake said, clinging to Jesse.

'Tis a bad omen, Iggywig be a-thinking.' He clung to the Dragon Hunter, who tried to shake him free from his sword arm. 'Me be a-shaking in my little booties.'

'Get off me,' the Dragon Hunter said.

The soft sand beneath Jesse sank two feet. She leapt back, Jake yelled. A swift hand shot out of the sand and grabbed his ankle. More sand gave way. Two more fast hands grabbed Jesse's ankles. Another seized Jake's free leg. Before the Dragon Hunter could shake Iggywig free from his sword arm, the children were pulled under, vanished beneath the sand.

'Get off!' The Dragon Hunter threw Iggywig down. He unleashed his sword of light.

100

The gobbit hit the sand with a dull thwack and tried to scramble to his feet. But he wasn't quick enough. A split second later he was yanked beneath the sand with electric speed.

The Dragon Hunter sheathed his sword, dropped to his knees, and dug frantically with his bare hands. Cyren used his huge feet to scrape away loads of sand. His feet were like enormous paddles. Kumo Diaz and Trondian-Yor sank to their knees and began their own frantic dig. With Cyren's help, within less than a minute, they had dug a hole big enough for four men to stand in.

'Save your energy,' Zarlan-Jagr said. He pointed ahead of them, to the rippling curve of the distant rim. 'Whatever has taken them is no longer here.'

'Let us help them,' the Dragon Hunter said. 'Use your magic.'

'If we use magic now our scent will be detected,' Trondian-Yor said. 'There is no cover out here. The element of surprise will be lost.'

'I do not think the element of surprise is with us any longer,' Zarlan-Jagr said. 'Our situation has left us with little choice.'

The Dragon Hunter got to his feet and brushed himself down. He, Iggywig, and Kumo Diaz mounted Cyren. With enormous flaps of its wings it rose into the air. They gave chase.

The two wizards flew into the sky like bullets, over taking them, swift in pursuit.

*

'What is it, sister dear?'

Dendrith's face broke into a smirk of pleasure. Her eyes were glazed. She had received telepathic communications from some unseen source. She nodded. She looked into the distant sky, towards the mountains. Her smirk widened into a hideous smile.

Her face darkened with a morose pleasure.

'Sister? What is it?'

'We hunt now,' Dendrith said calmly. She launched herself into the air. 'We have them. They have broken cover.'

The Driths swept into the pale blue-white sky. Jagdrith was close behind her mother. Their black cloaks billowed and flapped. They were like missiles locked onto their targets.

'To our enemies' deaths,' Gwendrith yelled, ghost-wasps spewing from her mouth.

'Kill them all,' Kildrith saluted.

Dendrith's mouth twisted into a grimace.

*

Zarlan-Jagr didn't know which way to look first. Beneath him, emerging from the sand, he saw Jesse, Jake and Iggywig. They were on their hands and knees gasping for breath. They had been spewed out where the desert finished and the lush inclined slopes began to rise into the snow-capped mountains. Ahead, to his left and right the Brood gathered in hundreds – a little higher up the slope. He knew that when they decided to move from their static position, they would soon be here. They were not far away, perhaps five hundred yards. Their monotone battle-cry echoed throughout the mountains, echoed in his ears. They banged the rocks around them like drums with their fists. Behind them, as he turned, he could see the dark flying figures of the Driths. There was nothing left but the battle ahead and the battle behind. He was thinking quickly about all the alternatives open to him. Of course, he was already dead – a spirit-wizard able to perform major league magic. But he feared for the mortality of his companions. The forces gathering around them now were far greater than him. He knew this, and accepted it. It was the way of things. It had already been foreseen many years ago. This day, this situation, this prelude to what was inevitable on the slopes of the Dead End Mountains had already been prophesised by one far wiser than the ascended Zarlan-Jagr. It was perhaps to become a defining glorious moment in the future myths and legends the Fairy Kingdoms held so dear. It was already part of one of the greatest Elriadian myths of the past, but perhaps soothsaying and reality might differ. He hoped the prophecy of Overstrand's Ancient Wizard of Elriad proved to be worthy, proved to be true. If not, then they would all be damned, and the Union of Thirteen would cease to exist as a force for great good, and would become a terrible force of evil.

He glanced down at Jesse, as she scrambled drunkenly to her feet. She was their best last chance, their best last hope. And ironically, the wizard thought, she doesn't even know it.

*

Jesse Jameson got up on wobbly legs and tried to steady herself against a boulder. She wiped rough sand from her face and shook lots of grains from her hair. She was gasping, eyes white and wide and frightened. She had a vivid memory of her journey beneath the sand. She recalled the insidious creatures which had dragged her into their mole-like tunnels. Pointed furry snouts, warm gripping hands, beady rat eyes, whiskers, hind-legs like scoops. They had seemed somehow partly human which disturbed her. She would later come to realise that what had scared her the most was the human warmth of their hands. It was the last thing she'd expected.

They had been trying to steal, or un-merge, the

obsidian Seeing-Stone which was now part of her flesh and bone. But in the brief encounter beneath the sand, her mind had been an explosion of snatched images, wayward thoughts, and deep dark dread.

There had been dozens of them and they had communicated in low grunts. One had sealed her lips and nose with a fine mesh. Another had somehow inserted a tube into her mouth so that she could breathe. Others had pulled her through the sand tunnels like an engine pulling subway carriages. All the time they had tried to pull out the obsidian stone from her hand, but they had failed. She had fought her instinct to scream only because her attention had been focused on breathing in through the tube, which she now remembered had been attached to a small canister clasped to her chest by one of the creature's hands. Grunts inside her mind had communicated a single sentence: *if you struggle, you will suffocate and die.* We do not want to harm you. But we do want the stone.

I have died before, she had said in her mind. But I don't want to again.

'Then give us the stone,' they had communicated.

I don't know how, she had thought.

She wondered if they believed her. It was the truth. She didn't know how the stone had been fused into her hand, and she certainly had no idea how to get it out again. The magic which she possessed was beyond her understanding. All of it. She didn't have a clue how it worked – except that wasn't completely true. She understood that her thoughts were powerful things. Perhaps some part of her brain had been accessed and then activated? Mrs Wobble had said on several occasions that only one-tenth of the brain was known about with some degree of certainty. Scientists didn't have all the answers. Maybe some part of the other nine-tenths had been tapped into somehow? Maybe. All she knew for certain was this: what she visualised in her mind's eye somehow transformed her body when shape-shifting, or unleashed powerful magic when using her firearm which had merged with the obsidian Seeing-Stone. But how? What were the mechanics? She didn't know.

The sand creatures stopped struggling to extract the stone. They had read her mind. She was telling the truth. It was the briefest of encounters. But they did not let her leave them empty-handed, for one of their kind submerged long needle-sharp fangs into Jesse's exposed neck. She winced at the momentary prick of pain.

Then her express journey beneath the sand ended suddenly. The vampire withdrew its bloody fangs. The coarse stinging sand erupted into blazing light, sharp mountains, lush green slopes. Mesh and tube and canister had been ripped from her by callous hands. As quickly as they came, the sand creatures were gone.

Jesse breathed in white-hot air and coughed. She spluttered. It hurt her lungs to breathe, filled her with a new dread. With the desert at her back, and the mountains angling before her, she stepped onto the slope and faced the Skaardrithadon's hoardes, who were standing like a dark fog some way up the slope. She couldn't block out their battle cry: 'Eal-gan-thaw! Eal-gan-thaw! Eal-gan-thaw! Eal-gan-thaw! Eal-gan-thaw!'

She wondered what it meant.

*

Jesse absently touched her punctured neck with the tips of her fingers. Her skin felt sticky and warm.

She withdrew her fingers and stared at them. Blood covered the tips. She shook involuntarily, her legs rubbery. She could feel something alien racing through her body. It was as if her arteries and veins were coursing with tiny sparks of electricity. She tingled inside her skin. She knew that the vampire's DNA had been injected into her blood stream and she wanted desperately to claw at it like an itch. But that of course was impossible. This itch was everywhere, all at once. This itch was unreachable with fingernails. But still she itched her skin, trying to bring some relief. She had to do something. Anything. Her heart raced at the thought of helplessness. Surely there was something she could do to stop the onset of becoming a vampire?

'Stop itching, you'll make your skin bleed,' Zarlan-Jagr said.

'I can't,' she said, in honesty. 'It's driving me mad.'

'Stop itching,' he said again. 'You have not been infected with vampire DNA. Remember what I told you. Only a Vampire Lord has the power of transformation.'

'If I have not been infected with vampire DNA, then what's happening to me?' Jesse said, itching wildly.

'You're suffering the side effects of a half-vampire who has sipped your blood.'

'Sipped my blood?'

'That's right. There was not enough time for a full drink.'

Jesse shuddered at the thought of the creature's needle-sharp fangs buried deep into her flesh, drinking from her. Full or not, it made her skin creep. Goosebumps erupted across her body.

'Yes, just a sip. That is all. It will pass.'

'That's all?' Jesse's head felt woozy. 'You make it sound like a cold.'

'It is less harmful than that. It will pass. Think of it like a nettle sting. It hurts terribly at first but soon passes.'

'How long does it take?'

'Not long, Jesse. Be patient. It will pass.'

'Okay, okay,' she said snappily. She itched her arms absently. At least the itching was letting up somewhat. 'I get the message. It will pass.'

But the truth of the matter hurt her. Whether it passed quickly or not, Jesse felt unclean. Something alien had invaded her body and the awful memory of it would be with her forever.

She saw Iggywig and Jake brushing themselves down. Iggywig smiled, Jake vomited.

'It's okay, Jake,' she said, detesting herself, because she knew it would never be okay. She untied the hide water-bag from her belt. 'Would you like some water?'

Jake took the container from her gingerly, straightening his body slowly. He swilled out his mouth and spat into the sand. Jesse said nothing about the waste of water. She watched him drink. He handed the container back to her. She took a little slurp and offered Iggywig a drink.

Raising his hand, he said, 'be a-kind offerings, Jesse, but Iggywig be a-no needing it just now.'

Jesse nodded and re-tied the bag to her waist. 'Did they harm you?' she said.

'No,' they both replied in unison.

'Thank Boeron for that,' she said, absently touching her neck. Unclean, alien, awful.

She suddenly noticed with growing alarm that the chanting had stopped. The silence was worse than the noise.

107

*

'They will attack us,' the Dragon Hunter said, his sword of light already buzzing in his hand. 'What do we do next?'

Zarlan-Jagr quickly shifted realities. He was in the magpie's mind now, and he flew up high in search of the Skaardrithadon. He'd had a feeling that the Vampire Lord might be on the move with Perigold and the rest of the Union of Thirteen. No, it was more than a feeling. It was a telepathic communication from a few of the members whose vampire transformations were not so advanced. And there was the proof, to the east, a huddle of dark cloaks winding their way up the side of the mountain toward the valley beyond the peak. He shifted back to his spirit-wizard self.

'If we fight here, we will die for no purpose,' he said, ignoring the fact that he was already dead. 'The Vampire Lord has moved the members of the Union.'

'Where to?' Trondian-Yor said.

'He's heading toward Death Valley.'

'What's there?' Jesse said, suddenly answering her own question in her mind. 'The Vampire Vault?'

Zarlan-Jagr nodded. 'So legend says. But where exactly is anyone's guess.'

'So we run again?' the Dragon Hunter said tersely, sheathing his sword.

'You may stay and fight, if you wish,' Zarlan-Jagr said. 'But we fly. Eastward. We must stop them before they reach the Vampire Vault.'

But it was too late. The attack had already begun.

Ten

Riders of Death Valley

Zarlan-Jagr was the first to react. He glanced up at the hundreds of creatures charging down the hillside and launched into them. He flew like a missile with his arms outstretched, but instead of forming fists to strike, he issued wave upon wave of blue-white pulsating light. From the foothills hundreds of mottled creatures were knocked clean over. But his magic could not defeat them all. The second and third platoons were soon swelling the attackers' ranks. One reached out as he swerved to miss a jutting rock and grabbed his leg, yanking him down to the ground with a sickening thump. The spirit-wizard couldn't believe it. These insubstantial creatures were spirits, too, and in such a state they both felt solid to one another.

He landed amongst them and fought. As if a gunfighter, he shot magic from his wriggling fingertips. But still they came at him, from every side now. He swivelled with a great turn of speed, so fast that his body became a blur. The spirit-wizard shoved one away, another grabbed his arm. A blow hit the side of his head. Rivers of pain washed through him. He kicked the creature away. More attacked. He ducked, dodged, plunged and dived. They clawed and snarled, scratched and shredded him with spite in each and every blow. He parried two punches aimed at his head, side-stepped a third blow, blocked a fourth with his arm. He twisted to his left one hundred and eighty degrees to face another barrage of creatures. They snarled and spat, eyes wild with rage. A half dozen dragged him down. He got to his feet. The creatures hounded him, dragged him down again. He got up. He blasted several to his right. They hit the rocky soil and did not move.

Zarlan-Jagr would have wiped sweat from his brow if he'd been flesh and blood. There are too many, he thought, his reactions instinctive now, inbred. He issued streams of light-pulsing magic from his fingertips and they fell – three, four, six, ten. Dozens crashed down, screamed, wild, becoming wilder before they twisted in agony all piled high around him.

He span to his right again as three creatures dived toward him from a rock which rose twelve feet above him. He waved his hand in an arc and a golden energy field erupted around him. The diving creatures hit it with a crunching-splitting sound and evaporated before his eyes. The energy field collapsed.

More creatures ran down from the foothills. Zarlan-Jagr weaved in and out of them as best he could, shooting magic from his fingers that stunned some and paralysed a few more. But these creatures were different, stronger than any other he had fought against. He changed his tactics now.

He flew on, upwards through the swarms of

creatures, but they were overpowering him. There were simply too many. He shook them off, hurtling into the sky. There were too many. Their defiant victorious war-cries echoed in his ears.

Ahead, swooping into the valley, he could see the distant silhouettes of his companions in the sky. Jesse led the way, with Kumo Diaz on her dragon back. Iggywig was close behind. Jake and the Dragon Hunter sat astride Cyren. The Driths were following them. Fast.

He felt something stirring the air waves. He turned his head and looked. Behind him, flying stealthily, were the giant bats from the Skaardrithadon's lair. He scanned the mountainside ahead. But he could not see the huddle of dark cloaks winding their way up the mountainside as before. The Skaardrithadon and the Union members had gone. Vanished. And there was another danger. Beyond, moving like a storm through the distant valley's undergrowth thundered the Riders. His spirit heart sank, fluttered. The odds were overwhelming. But he knew what he would have to do. The Ancient Wizard of Elriad's prophesy was reaching its climax. So that Jesse and the rest could follow the Skaardrithadon, attempt to unleash the Curse of Caldazar, I will stand and fight for all eternity if needs be.

He focused his eyes on the approaching Riders and dropped like a falcon toward them.

*

Jesse glanced down from her vantage point in the sky and saw the great dark blot on the landscape hurrying closer and closer. They came on horseback. Or at least looking down on them the creatures they rode upon resembled horses. There were so many of them that their shouts and the thud of hooves sounded like a summer flash-flood storm. They cut up the valley floor, kicking up sods and grass and dirt. The soil was damp so there were no dust clouds. But way below, in the bottom of the valley, Jesse heard the noise of their coming echo horribly. It was a deep thumping cacophony. They were the Riders – that's what the local half-vampire's called them. They were splattered from head to toe with dirty brown mud. But still their red eyes glowed with frightening clarity.

Jesse glanced to her left and saw the Skaardrithadon and a huddle of dark cloaks veer into a small cave entrance half way up the mountain. As she turned to follow, she heard Iggywig cry out.

She turned her dragon head and saw the gobbit thrashing, writhing in the sky like a victim of a bird of prey. It was Kildrith. The warlock had Iggywig locked in his arms and they plummeted toward the rocks below, fighting.

She did not see Zarlan-Jagr blast into the Riders like an exploding bomb. There was a silent flash of white-blue light. Instead, Jesse's eyes were honed on the other Driths, who were circling, buzzing menacingly around Cyren. The Dragon Hunter had unleashed his sword of light. Jake screamed, cowered, grabbing Cyren's neck, keeping low as the Dragon Hunter's sword flashed this way and that. The Driths hissed and spat.

'They're after Jake,' Jesse said. 'We have to help them. Without him the Curse of Caldazar will be useless.'

Kumo Diaz smirked wickedly behind her back. His hand was resting on his knife handle. 'What about poor Iggywig. Look. His need seems greater right now.'

Jesse looked down at the tumbling mass of wings and dark cloak. They seemed oblivious to the approaching rocks and their certain deaths.

'Iggywig needs you more,' Kumo Diaz said. 'Hurry before it's too late.'

Jesse glanced at the Dragon Hunter, who was holding his own with the Driths for the time being. Kumo Diaz was right, she thought. Iggywig needed her more right now. She twisted and turned, folding her wings so that her bullet shape dropped at a tremendous speed.

'Fly up!' she yelled in a roaring deep dragon bellow. Her voice rumbled the air like thunder. 'Iggywig! For Boeron's sake, FLY UP!'

The gobbit and the warlock tumbled down ever closer to the rocks below.

*

Zarlan-Jagr hit the first Riders like a storm-force wave. He bowled them over. With the wave of energy that rushed out seconds before his arrival.

They toppled over backwards, crashing into the next surge of Riders. The horse-like creatures they rode upon wailed and rolled backwards, too. The on-coming Riders were thrown from their mounts by the tumbling creatures.

Zarlan-Jagr landed on his two nimble feet and stood his ground, knee-deep in mud. He lassoed them with whipping, slashing forks of lightning. He shot the magic from his searing palm. His fingertips were on fire. But he didn't seem to notice the cork-screws of blue smoke that drifted from them.

Still they rode out of the valley toward him. Their numbers were many, riding fast and deep. Steam and snot poured from the nostrils of the creatures they rode.

'Your formidable reputation is bigger than you are

113

in reality,' he said beneath his breath to them. Then louder. 'Legend has lied yet again. You are all dark cloaks and thundering noise. You shall not ride by me this day.'

They rode harder toward him, screaming from inside their dark hoods.

He raised his hands in a high circle, zigzag lightning still pouring from his fingertips. He shook his hands toward them, as if shaking water from soaking palms. Thousands of bullet-sized light particles sprayed them, as if a machine gun had let loose an entire magazine. The Riders screamed, fell, retreated under the power of the spirit-wizard's superior magic.

One moment they seemed up for the battle, the next they'd turned, thundering back up the valley, and melted into the shadows again.

After they had dragged their dead and wounded into the depths of the dark places they had emerged from, Zarlan-Jagr turned to look toward the battle in the sky.

*

Iggywig tumbled, wrestling free of Kildrith just seconds before they would hit the rocks. Spinning uncontrollably from the force of their battle, Kildrith was disorientated. He tried to fly upward, but his mind was confused. Instead he sped faster toward the rocks.

Seconds before he smashed his beaten body on a jutting rock, Jesse Jameson swooped down and grabbed Iggywig. She held him with her dragon jaws and climbed the air currents slowly, her wings beating in a huge powerful rhythm. In the distance, a little further up the valley, she saw a beautiful sight. Hundreds of waterfalls were cascading from the mountainside into white-water rivers and tributaries, gushing, frothing wildly, crashing against rising boulders and jutting ridges, joining another calmer river, which was wide and meandering and peaceful.

Kildrith hit the rocks with a dull thud. His dark cloak fluttered like a flag of defeat. His broken body was motionless.

Jesse glanced back, lost in memories briefly. She recalled the fear Kildrith had instilled in her as they'd battled in Rainley's churchyard, or the horror as he'd stepped out of the shadows in Loath Town to reveal his ruined face. He'd pursued her to his death. He looked so tiny and alone down there. She wondered if anyone would grieve for him. Did he have a mother or father who loved him? She didn't know. She felt a little sympathy for him momentarily, but it was soon gone. He had been a dark evil thing, and that fact she couldn't forget however sad his death. He had hunted her relentlessly in both the human world and the fairy kingdoms. He had been bad.

As she rose higher into the sky, scanning for the Dragon Hunter, Jake and Cyren, she felt an awful sense of foreboding. Where were they? And where were the Driths?

*

Zarlan-Jagr was about to launch himself into the sky, but he was assailed by a wave of giant bats. In the heat of battle with the Riders he'd forgotten about them. Now these creatures were no push over. They were experts of the air, and encircled him like a squadron of dark fighter planes. He desperately wanted to fly up and help Jesse, but he would be no match for the bats. Their numbers were large and their aerial skills far greater than his. He feared his speed alone would not be enough to shake them.

Besides, he would lead them straight to Jesse and the Vampire Vault. For now in the hazy fading twilight he saw the Driths flying toward the Vault's mountainside entrance. They had their prisoners in tow, Jake, the Dragon Hunter, and Trondian-Yor. More of the prophecy had unravelled itself.

*

Jesse Jameson glimpsed her companions vanishing into the dark entrance on the side of the mountain. Iggywig was conscious and riding on her dragon back. He was behind Kumo Diaz. He was a little groggy, still light-headed from his experience, but basically in good shape.

'No,' Jesse said, shaking her head. 'They've been captured.'

'Not all,' said Kumo Diaz. 'Over there. See?'

Jesse rotated her head and saw Cyren flying away into the distance.

'Where's he going?' Jesse said.

'Tis Iggywig's humble opinionings that brave Cyren be a-going for more helpings.'

'We could do with some help,' Jesse said, swooping toward the dark mouth of the cave where her friends had disappeared.

'Yes, help would be good,' the tracker said.

His grip tightened on the knife handle.

*

Zarlan-Jagr bowed his head in respect. So this was the moment of change, the moment vampire flesh and blood would be made, unmade and remade. The Great Unbalancing was once again swinging like a pendulum, back and forth, back and forth. He hoped with all his heart that the Ancient Wizard of Elriad's prophecy were true, otherwise those who would sacrifice themselves this day would be sacrificed in the name of darkness and evil. But

116

his part in this affair was over now. He knew this with the certainty of one who knew when it was time to walk away, not because of a lack of courage or a cold heart but because it was the way it had to be. Yes, my part in this story is over now.

'It's up to you, Jesse Jameson,' he said. 'Your time has come. You are on your own, soothsayer, shape-shifter. Do not fail. Let the Seeing-Stone guide you.'

And the spirit-wizard's cloak tumbled gently onto the mud, an empty cloth. He would never return to the Vampire lands again.

Eleven

Vampire Vault

They landed on a narrow ledge. It jutted out a few feet behind them. Less than four steps away beckoned the darkness of the cave's mouth. Below, the mountain face was sheer and harsh. The valley was a long, long way below that. A fall from this height would end in a terrible death.

As Jesse Jameson transformed into her fairy self, Kumo Diaz unsheathed the knife.

'A good idea,' Jesse said to the tracker. 'What weapon have you got, Iggywig?'

Iggywig wriggled his fingers and produced a long crystal stake. 'Be a-needing this Iggywig thinks to be a-plunging into the Vampire Lord's heart.'

'Er ... right?' Jesse said, thinking of the vampire myths she knew from the human kingdom. Could it be that simple? 'What about the Curse?'

'Tis a good to be a-saying the Curse. But we be a-needing Jake, too.' He held the stake up a little higher. 'This be backup.'

Jesse smiled and then her face furrowed seriously. 'We'll get Jake out of here. And we'll help

118

the others escape, too. Right, Kumo?'

'Wrong,' said Kumo Diaz. 'This is where it ends.'

'What?' Jesse couldn't hide her confusion. At first she thought that the tracker had been joking. But the way he motioned the blade toward her did not look like the actions of a joker. His eye showed no flicker of emotion. It was hard, no impossible to read him.

'You're a fool, Jesse Jameson,' he said harshly. 'You don't stand a chance. The Skaardrithadon will snap you in two just like that.' He clicked his fingers and smirked. He motioned with the blade toward the entrance. 'Now, walk. That way. I've a delivery to make.'

'A delivery?'

'Stop being so thick, Jesse Jameson. Can't you see what's happening? It's right before your eyes. I've delivered you to the Vampire Lord.'

'But why?'

'Why betray you?' His voice was bleak, almost raging.

'Yes, why betray-'

'Shut up and listen! You might learn something.' He had a point to make, but shouting wouldn't make her listen. He paused, deliberately softening his voice. She had to understand. Perhaps it would ease her transformation as a full vampire after the Skaardrithadon had taken a bite. 'Remember the Battle for Caldazar?'

'How could I forget?'

'Remember how I refused to fight in that War?'

'Yes,' she said. 'You left us there in that enormous hangar at Stinkburrow.'

'I left because I hate war.'

'You said it was complicated, that you were a simple tracker.'

119

'Well done,' he said sarcastically. 'You were listening. Yes, I am a simple tracker. But you fairy folk have never left me alone to do what I love. There's always been someone – usually Zarlan-Jagr – tracking *me* down to do the Union a favour. A little tracking job here, a little tracking job there. Well, I'm sick of the Thirteen clicking their fingers and me running like a dog to their beck and call.'

'I'm sure Zarlan-Jagr has never-'

'Don't tell me what Zarlan-Jagr has or hasn't done, child.' He waved the knife close to her face. 'I'm sick of the sermons from his kind – *your* kind. I have slaved for him for more years than I care to recall. But not anymore. Now I have delivered you to the Vampire Lord, I'll be ...'

His voice trailed away. A new glint, a knowing sparkle lit his single wide compound eye. 'Why am I telling you this? My plans have nothing to do with either of you.' He glared at Iggywig. He jerked his head toward the cave. 'Just get in there and let's get this over and done with.'

'I can't let you take us prisoner,' Jesse said.

Kumo Diaz laughed. 'I know. But you have no choice.' He slipped around and behind the gobbit with silky speed. He grabbed Iggywig around the throat, sliding the blade under the gobbit's neck. 'But if you attempt to use your shape-shifting powers or that damn Seeing-Stone fused into your hand, then I'll cut his throat. How does that sound?'

''Tis bad,' Iggywig said, gulping.

'Okay,' Jesse said, lying like a wizard. 'We'll do it your way. What next?'

'You go first,' the tracker said. 'Any tricks and he dies.'

'I understand,' she said, walking into the darkness of the cave's mouth. She transformed the split second she entered the dark. She became the Wild Winds of Murokchi. She was instantly invisible. The tracker edged inside the cave, gripping Iggywig's throat tightly.

Jesse attacked before Kumo Diaz's eye could accustom itself to the dark. She entered his ear, wispy, cold, seeking. In seconds she was coursing through his outer ear canal, along his middle and inner ear; and on deeper into the hidden eustachian tube. Riding atop the inner ear she rushed into the semi-circular canals, which helped maintain his balance.

It happened so fast that the tracker was aware only of his swaying dizziness. He let go of Iggywig and staggered sideways out of the cave onto the ledge. Inside his head he heard the Wild Winds of Murokchi chanting his name over and over. He dropped the knife, clutched his hands to his ears, still desperate to gain his balance.

Jesse hurtled around and around inside his inner semi-circular canals. He could not regain his balance, sidling crab-like toward the brink of the ledge. He tried to lean forward but he staggered like a drunk, stepping over the edge and plummeting down toward the rocks below.

Jesse swirled out of his ear the same way she'd entered and transformed into a giant bat. She caught him in her claws, steering him away from the rocks and settled him down on an outcrop many thousands of feet from the cave's mouth. He cursed her and her kind as she flew swiftly back to the ledge. Landing, she transformed into her fairy self. She glanced down. He was a tiny speck amidst the peaks of snow. Both he and the peaks were silhouettes now in the last vestiges of stretched twilight. She could not hear his insults. He was too far away.

She walked into the cave's mouth.

Behind her she did not see the searing flesh sky. Low on the darkening horizon a broad black cloud of bats rose silently from their hidden roosts. It was too late now.

Jesse stepped slowly into the dark vault. It was enormous – more a cathedral than a vault. Its size made her heart race. Her footfalls echoed like explosions as she walked along the narrow pathway. Below her, on either side was nothing but blackness and certain death. To her left, fixed to the walls, she saw giant torches upturned like vampires' teeth. Purple flames flickered as if snake tongues. Somewhere in the distance, deep inside the vault, she could hear a constant hiss, as though a hosepipe had sprung a leak.

As her eyes got used to the dark she saw silhouetted coffins. They were closed and upright. Row upon row lined the walls. They were stacked at least one hundred high and a thousand deep.

'Vampires,' she gasped. 'Thousands of vampires.'

'These be no ordinary vampires. Tis the mythological resting place of the Vampire Lords.'

'Yes,' Jesse said, feeling numb. So at last they had managed to arrive, despite all the obstacles. Her cheeks glowed hot and sticky. Her heart beat increased.

'Tis a bad placing we be,' Iggywig whispered. He was trembling. 'Be a-wise to be a-turning back.'

'We can't,' Jesse said, trying to sound as brave as she could. Her voice crackled with fear. 'We have to stay and face them.'

Iggywig turned to run, but Jesse gripped his arm. She was stronger than she'd thought. The gobitt winced, yelped a little in pain.

'Magic, Iggywig. We have plenty of it between us. We must use it. We must fight.'

Iggywig stopped his retreat and nodded. He clutched the magic crystal stake in one hand and rubbed his aching arm with the other. 'Iggywig be a-sorrying, Jesse. Forgive me. Fear be our enemy.'

'Yes,' Jesse said, letting go of his arm and gripping her own glistening stake. 'Fear be our enemy.'

On wobbling legs, they slowly inched forward along the narrow, winding pathway deeper into the vault. They did not look down on either side. The abyss was wide and black.

Twenty feet above them, at a forty-five degree angle, Jesse noticed it first and Iggywig a split second later: a dark gargoyle perched like a crow on a sloping red roof. The gargoyle twitched and flapped its leathery wings. Little zigzags of mauve and blue fork-lightning flashed as each wing tip touched. A second of silence was shattered by an electrifying boom of thunder. Red eyes glowed like hot coals and simmered to pale embers.

'Wait until it makes its move,' Jesse said.

'Tis an idea you be a-having, brave Jesse?'

'Yes, but you'll have to trust me, Iggywig. I think the gargoyle can hear every word we say.'

'Be no doubting,' Iggywig said. 'Gargoyles be a-known for their unnatural sensings.'

The gargoyle snarled, unfurling its black lips like a flag. It jumped up, sidled about five feet, stopped and hunched its shoulders. Suddenly it seemed aware of them or the cold coffins gawping at its neck. It turned slowly, sniffing the humid air. Wind rattled the empty rafters. The gargoyle edged slowly along the roof.

'Turn back,' it hissed. 'Or I will kill you.'

Iggywig tilted his head, and looked up at the gargoyle. 'Be a-brave wording you be a-saying, foul creature. We be a-meaning you no harmings,' he said.

'Turn back or you die,' it repeated.

Jesse did not move, but felt the obsidian fused in her palm tingle magically. Her hand was on fire – red, orange, yellow, glowing to purple.

The gargoyle nodded as if he had known it all along. 'What magic you possess in your hand is useless here. You'll die before you use it!'

'We shall see,' she said calmly.

Jesse Jameson opened her glowing palm and held up her hand as if stopping traffic. Sparks erupted and she trembled with the force of the magic coursing through her body.

It was then that the thousands of coffin doors crashed open. From green clouds of mist a multitude of white-faced vampires stepped out with eyes blazing red revenge and malice.

Jesse's jaw dropped open.

Iggywig fainted.

'Get up,' Jesse said, bending, slapping Iggywig's face. 'Get up.'

The gobbit half-opened his eyes slowly. At first he saw only Jesse's anxious eyes, and then looming like a boom he saw thousands of burning crimson eyes – distant now, but not for long. They were coming. He closed his eyes, rubbed them in disbelief, opened them again to more disbelief. He sat up like a bolt, drew his breath in sharply, and exhaled, puffing out his cheeks. To Iggywig, Jesse's open palm was like a setting ruby-orange sun. He took her outstretched hand. It felt hot, glowed. She hauled him to his feet. He laughed in an insane jittery way.

More coffin doors creaked, squealed, crashed

open. Vampires everywhere! Vampires all around! Vampires! Everywhere! Run!

'Run!' he yelled, tugging Jesse.

'No,' she said.

'Yes.'

'No! We have come too far to turn back now.'

Iggywig shook his head, baffled. 'You be mad,' he said. 'Just be a-looking what we be up against.'

'Perhaps they will be slow,' she reasoned, grasping for an excuse not to retreat, grasping for anything. 'Perhaps they will be drowsy. They have slept for a long time.'

'Don't be a-looking drowsy to Iggywig.'

'But the others need us. We can't abandon them, to let them become full vampires.'

'You have no choice in the matter, child,' came the chilling voice above her.

She glanced up. It was Perigold. He was standing next to the gargoyle. He was dressed in black from head to toe. His eyes looked bright-wild even in the dim light.

So, she was too late. He was a vampire now. Lost.

'Too late,' she muttered under her breath.

Perigold smiled, a twisted smile which made him look sinister and much younger. 'Yes, too late,' he said. 'Your journey is a wasted one.'

'Are you ...' Her voice trailed away. She couldn't say it. The thought was too awful. 'A full vampire?'

Speechless. Dumfounded. Mouth ajar. The pause was filled with drama, a chilling dark dramatic stop that poured dread into her heart. She knew the answer already. She could see the hideous result of the Skaardrithadon's DNA right before her.

'Yes, I am a full vampire,' he said.

'No,' she said weakly, feeling her knees buckle. 'And the others?'

'They are no longer your concern. It's over. The Union of Thirteen exists no more. It is a dark order now. Leave while you can.'

Leave while you can? Jesse thought. Why would he say that if he were a full vampire? Surely he would want to gain the Skaardrithadon's favour, not do her a favour? Perhaps he wasn't a full vampire after all. Perhaps – yes that was it – Perigold was just pretending. Perhaps his own DNA had transmuted the vampire DNA, and now he had a plan to free them all? Yes, this was part of his plan to free the Union members, the Dragon Hunter, and Jake. Why else would he tell them to go?

'Be a wise wordings to leave,' Iggywig said. 'This place be a-giving me the creepy crawlings. See?' He held out his trembling hands to demonstrate his fear.

'Okay,' Jesse said. 'Let's leave.'

'What?' Iggywig couldn't believe his ears.

'Come on,' she said, taking his hand. 'It's over. Let's go.'

They started to walk quickly back the way they had come. More full vampires were waking, doors crashing open, hinges squealing, echoing in the vast vault. They hurried their pace. Not much further to the entrance. The soft flesh sky was pink and warm, the sun almost disappearing beyond the horizon. Inviting. Oh how the light invited them. And there was still enough of it to make their way for awhile, once out in the open. The air out there was mildly scented with honeysuckle fragrance.

They broke into a trot.

Howling mock laughter rang someway ahead of them.

Twelve

Over the Edge

The Skaardrithadon stepped out from the shadows into the backlit threshold of the entrance. He blocked the way before them.

My God, Jesse thought, mesmerized by his slicked-back black hair. Just like her first encounter with him in the Innermost Sanctum his harsh white face made his large black eyes look abnormally large. He was a giant, standing fully eight feet tall. His lips were thin but no longer blood-red. They were black, twisted. His long black cloak and black knee-length leather boots glimmered like polished coal; shone a dull light of their own. His cloud wafted like an evening mist around his legs and waist, bathing him in effervescence.

He opened his cloak like bats wings and from beneath them Jake tumbled out of one side, and the Dragon Hunter out of the other. They crouched on their haunches, wide-eyed, brooding, gazing around the vault in bewilderment.

Jesse felt her heart lurch, ache as if a hammer had missed a nail and hit her thumb. This was awful. The Dragon Hunter and Jake? Both on their way to becoming vampires? And she had been betrayed by her own grandfather, too. It really was all too much. She felt sick inside, numb, shocked.

She re-aligned her thoughts. No – not her own grandfather. He was gone now. This, this thing above her perched on the roof was someone different, *something* different. It was a wicked, evil shadow of her loving grandfather.

Perigold leapt down from the roof onto the narrow ledge of the precipice. He moved swiftly up behind them, smirking darkly. 'Did you like my little joke, my Lord?' he said.

'It amused me for a moment, Perigold. Thank you. You may leave us now.'

'Yes, my Lord.'

He hissed his subservience and turned on his heel, his shoes squeaking mouse-like. He hurried into the darkness. He did not glance over his shoulder at Jesse. He had gone. She had been too late. The vampire DNA had taken control. She shook her head slowly, trying to take in the nightmare.

'So glad you could join our little gathering,' the Skaardrithadon said, his voice thick with irony. He patted his new pet, the Dragon Hunter, on his head. The Dragon Hunter winced, flinched, looked up balefully at his new master.

'This is a great night for our people,' the Vampire Lord said, motioning toward the opening coffins.

'Where are the others?' Jesse said.

The Skaardrithadon ignored her question and ruffled Jake's hair, mocking playfulness. 'Yes, a new era is dawning for the vampires. A glorious one. Once more we will hold sway over all the domains and kingdoms. Once again we will walk the streets without fear of persecution, bullying, and harassment. We are a noble breed and all shall bow to our nobility.'

'Where are Trondian-Yor and the rest of the Union members?'

The Skaardrithadon locked his hypnotic eyes on her. His face darkened, not by any change of the light in dim vault, but by something crawling and evil beneath the Vampire Lord's pale flesh. 'You are wasting my time with your questions. There is no way past. It is over for you and the Union of Thirteen. See how your loyal friends have deserted you? They are loyal to me now.'

She gazed down at the Dragon Hunter and Jake. They hissed at her like crazed wild cats, exposing fangs. She drew back a little, concerned they would attack. So it was true – he had them all except her, Iggywig and Zarlan-Jagr. She wondered briefly where the spirit-wizard might be, gazing hopefully around the vault. All she saw was the myriad ledges crammed with awakening vampires. Blazing blue light back-lit them. It shone out strongly from within the coffins. Everywhere else within the huge cavernous vault, except for a few torches on the walls, was dark and submerged in deep rich velvety shadow.

'Let me past,' Jesse said again, a hard edge to her voice.

'No,' said the Skaardrithadon. He opened his cloak as if wings and clouds of silver mist poured from him. 'It is time to join us.'

He lurched forward, exposing fangs, hissing, eyes wider than ever.

Jesse leapt back, as if lightning had struck.

Iggywig pounced, leaping into the cloud, screaming like a wild beast. He held out the crystal stake like a spear. Jesse heard a thud – snarls, growls, yells, screams, fists pounding from within the thickening cloud.

She took her chance. She edged around the cloud, not looking down at the abyss which loomed either side of the narrow pathway. She moved closer now to the entrance, where the path widened. Afraid that he would slip into the abyss, she turned and yelled at Iggywig. Here was the opportunity.

'Let's go!' she yelled.

But a silence descended – eerie, thrumming, dark. The fighting had stopped. Alarm rasped her spine like a cat's tongue. She feared the worst for Iggywig. No, if truth be told she feared far worse than she could admit. She knew that any moment now she must use her magic – a magic she had been told never to use unless no other course of action could be taken. The time had come yet again. She could feel the strange force igniting inside her. Her obsidian Seeing-Stone tingled the flesh of her palm, growing hotter. The Skaardrithadon couldn't take Iggywig from her, too. She would do all in her power to stop him. He would take no more of her friends today.

The cloud broke open momentarily.

It was Jake. He was still crouching, a wildness in his eyes. He saw her. She saw him, his geeky face looking like a waif stranger.

'The Curse!' she yelled to him. 'Jake remember the Curse of Caldazar!'

For a moment, the light of recollection flared in his eyes. Jesse leaned over to him, to pull him from the cloud. She offered her hand.

'Yes, Jake, that's it,' she said. 'You remember, don't you?'

She reached out further.

'Take my hand, Jake. That's it.'

130

Jake looked at his fingers, looked up at Jesse's hand. The cloud threatened to close, billowed open once more.

'The Curse of Caldazar?' she said with more urgency now. 'Let's chant it together.'

Jake reached out his hand. His recollection was dawning. Yes, Jake, she thought. Yes, Jake. Yes, Jake. Yes!

Their fingertips touched.

As if fire had seared him, Jake withdrew his hand, winced. His own fingers were ice to Jesse, she drew back her own hand, shocked by the chill. Opposites now, in mind and flesh.

For a split second she saw old Jake, but it was too late. There would be no happy ending, no chanting, no curse to send the Skaardrithadon back whence he came.

Jake spat-hissed at her, hissed again. She wiped spittle from her cheek. 'I love you, Jake,' she said softly. 'Goodbye.'

Jake reared up at the words, stood taller than he'd ever stood in his short life. But then Iggywig flew backwards out of the cloud and hit the ground with a crunching thump. He was sprawled out on the narrow path, his left leg and arm dangling over the edge. If he shifted his weight that way he would fall into the abyss. Jake was pulled back into the mist by huge hands and the Skaardrithadon loomed like a tower above her. He laughed insanely.

'Join me, Jesse Jameson. Of your own free will. Do not resist. You have much to admire. The darkness is a glorious place to be. Join my crusade. We could make a wonderful team. I will make you a Vampire Princess.'

Jesse twisted away from him and hurried to Iggywig. She crouched down to tend to him. The gobbit was barely breathing. She cupped his head in her hands. She felt his neck. There were holes and blood there. She gasped a little, drew in a short breath of despair. She dragged him away from the edge, to a wider section of the path. Now he had taken Iggywig. His blood would be coursing with vampire DNA. Soon, perhaps hours, or maybe days, she wasn't sure, he would become just like the Skaardrithadon. The thought made her feel sick.

She looked up at the Vampire Lord.

'How could you?'

'He was a feisty little battler. He will make a fine addition to my ranks,' he said, nodding at him. He locked his eyes on her. 'So will you join me of your own free will? What is your answer to my offer?'

Something odd ripped inside Jesse, tore at her heart. Her anger subsided, faded. She felt his huge sadness, his huge pain, his huge emptiness. Did he truly believe that she could fill that void? That she would join him of her own free will? Or was he toying with her again, a sick vampire joke?

'You wonder what it would be like, don't you, Jesse?'

His voice was silky smooth, deep, alluring.

She tried to wrench her eyes from his hypnotic glare, but could not. She felt her eyes growing heavier, lids falling, legs wanting to walk, to walk into his cloud and join him.

'Yes, you want to taste the blood of fairy and human. That's it, isn't it?'

Yes, she said in her head.

'No!' she screamed at him. But her scream sounded different, a million miles away, distant.

'Don't lie to yourself, Jesse. Come, join me.'

The Vampire Lord held out his hand. His pale flesh shone like buffed ivory in the half-light.

'Join us,' he said. His voice was a magnet. 'You could be re-united with Jake, the Dragon Hunter, Perigold. Not to mention all the other members of the Thirteen. Wouldn't that be wonderful?'

'Yes,' she whispered hoarsely, eyes locked to his. She couldn't break away, didn't want to break away now.

Smooth as silk.

She stood up slowly, leaving Iggywig lying, breathless, moaning in pain on the ground. It felt like the right thing, the only thing to do. She stepped toward the cloud. Then something alien shimmered inside her. It was an opposite pole to the negativity of the Vampire Lord's powers of persuasion. It fluttered, butterfly-like, danced joyously, repaired her torn heart. Healing hands. Mighty hands. Soothing. Her head cleared, something inside her was breaking the Vampire Lord's spell. This silky soothing was like a warm breeze.

'Where are the members of the Union?' she said, without thinking. It just popped out. 'Where is Trondian-Yor?'

'Sleeping,' he said. 'You will meet them later.'

'Okay,' she said, lying like a wizard. 'What next?'

He offered his hand, certain he had her in his grasp. She reached out and gripped his strong hand. He pulled her toward the cloud.

She laughed, he frowned.

The searing heat from her obsidian palm ignited, fused his flesh to her flesh. They were sealed together as if by super glue.

He yanked, she squeezed.

He tried to release her burning palm but she was too strong. Ridiculous. She was just a child. How could this be?

133

'What illusion is this, fairy child?' he snapped.

She was dragging him out of his cloud like a mother dragging her screaming child to school.

'Let go. The heat is hurting me.'

Still Jesse dragged him from the shell of his cloud, like a snail picked by a hungry thrush.

'Release me! Do you hear?'

She heard but she wouldn't speak. His dominion was over. Whatever was inside her was powerful. This was not her magic alone. Someone else had united with her.

'Kill her!' the Skaardrithadon commanded.

His order was to anyone listening. The Vampire Lords stirring from their deep hibernation, emerging from coffins, were in no fit state to fight. Some stirred, tried to break free of a millennium of sleep, but with little success. The cloud around the Skaardrithadon was dissipating, revealing the Dragon Hunter and Jake. They snarled like dogs at their master's heel, but did no more than make noises.

Jesse needed answers. She continued to drag him closer. So where were Trondian-Yor and the captured eight members of the Union? Were they behind her incredible strength?

'Let go, you fairy scum!' the Vampire Lord yelled. 'Let go now!'

But she couldn't let go, even if she had wanted to. The obsidian Seeing-Stone was white hot, melting his hand, but she felt cool, calm, powerful.

The Driths appeared from the darkness. They had heard the Vampire Lord's call for help. They flew at her, howling and cursing. She raised her free hand. It glowed. They had felt the force of her firearm before, in the Innermost Sanctum back in Caldazar. They were not fools. Fickle hags, yes. But not fools

134

here today. Hissing, they backed away, flew off towards the cave entrance, muttering something about the impressive power of Jesse Jameson, able to reduce the New Master of Darkness to a gibbering baby, swearing at one another for their inept performance in gaining revenge, their pathetic attempt at extracting the golden glow.

'How do I reverse the vampire DNA you injected into my friends?' Jesse said.

'I don't know,' he said.

The heat became hotter. He screamed, dragged out completely from his cloud.

'Tell me,' she said.

'But I don't know.'

'You lie.'

'No.'

'Yes.'

More excruciating heat burned his flesh. She would not stop until he gave her what she wanted.

'I don't know. Let me go back to my cloud,' he said desperately, wincing.

'No.'

She dragged him closer still, his pallid face just inches from her now. He hissed, revealing needle-sharp fangs. She hissed back, unafraid. Her hand was like a naked flame on his flesh, like a vice crushing him. The harder she squeezed, the hotter it became. He screamed in agony.

'Tell me how to bring my friends back from their vampire hell.'

'I don't know of any way. No-one has reversed the vampire DNA. I wouldn't know where to begin. It's impossible. They are vampires now – forever!'

'You lie.'

'No, you lie to yourself. They cannot return.'

And there was a small glint of pleasure in his

eyes. He was telling the truth.

Jesse saw it and her own dark anger welled up inside, rose like flood frothing dirty waters on the verge of breaking the bank which held them. She dragged him screaming to the edge of the abyss. She lifted him up with her new strength, held him over the edge, staring dark death in the face. The deep unfathomable pit of darkness loomed all around them. She would cast him in. He had taken them all from her. Only a broken and wheezing Iggywig was left, and he would become a vampire sooner or later. It was over. Her life was ruined, her friends all gone. Taken by *him*!

She looked at him coldly. He was leaning backwards, feet scrambling against the crumbling edge of the pathway. She loathed him. Behind him the vast blackness beckoned. All she had to do was release him, reverse the flux which had melded their flesh together. Then he would tumble to his death.

'Don't do it,' the Vampire Lord said. 'Please.'

She glanced over her shoulder. Jake and the Dragon Hunter were still crouched on the floor. They were huddled together, drooling and bewildered, moving closer to the vampire state each second.

She clicked the fingers of her free hand and the Obsidian Container appeared.

'If Jake could say the Curse of Caldazar with me, then I'd send you back to where you came from. But that is impossible now. This thing is useless, isn't it?'

'Don't drop me.'

'It's been a waste of time tracking you. This thing is useless now.'

The Obsidian Container's tiny light was green. It was the closest she'd ever been to him, but its power of containment was useless now. Without Jake, the

136

Curse of Caldazar was just harmless words on her lips alone.

'Let me up. Don't drop me.'

Jesse stared at him with a bleak coldness in her eyes and released the Obsidian Container. It fell without sound into the abyss. She listened for the distant crash as it shattered on the bottom but the sound didn't come. The abyss was deeper, far deeper than she could have imagined.

Perigold appeared from the darkness, high on the roof where she'd first seen him. He was surrounded by the other members of the Union of Thirteen. Trondian-Yor stepped forward. His face was ashen, mouth twisted to expose his vampire fangs. He hissed at her. They all hissed at her, spat from on high.

'You've taken them all,' she said. She shook her head. 'How could you?'

'Please,' he said. 'Don't let me fall.'

Her anger swelled up in her heart again. All of her friends were gone now. He deserved to die for what he had done. But would he die? What if she released him and instead of dying he lived? What if the abyss was an escape? That's crazy, she told herself. If it was an escape route, a void to another time and place maybe, why was he so scared to fall?

'Jesse.'

She turned, spooked by the voice. It was Iggywig. He was raised up on an elbow, grimacing with pain.

'Yes, Iggywig,' she said. 'I will see what I can do for your pain soon.'

'Be no need for helpings,' he said breathlessly. 'Too late for Iggywig.' He touched his neck and raised his blood-coated fingers. 'Be a Full Vampire soon.'

'No,' she said weakly. It was too much to bear.

She looked the Skaardrithadon. 'You will pay now for what you have done.'

The fear slid momentarily from his face and he nodded. 'You will never stop us now. Kill me and another Lord will take my place. Look how many come now.'

She followed his gaze up to the thousands of Vampire Lords leaping down from the highest rows of coffins. There were so many of them, ancient, dark, brooding. More and more were waking. He was right, she hated to admit it.

'Which ever way you look at it,' he said, smiling smugly, 'vampires win, and the fairies lose. There are only the vampires now.'

She looked across at the entrance. A swelling crowd of vampires had blocked out the twilight. Perigold and Trondian-Yor, followed by the other Union members, leapt down from the roof. They joined the throng of Vampire Lord's now descending upon Jesse. Their primordial hissing grew louder and louder. Their dark eyes glowed with hatred for the fairy child.

'Once you've dropped me,' the Vampire Lord went on, 'they will rip you to shreds. You've no way out. Listen to reason. Unless I command them to back off, they will kill you. Let me up, release your grip. You have my word – let me live and I'll let you go free from here as a fairy. You are no real threat to us. Your kind will serve us soon enough. But if you wish it, you are free to leave. Pull me up.'

Jesse thought about the kind of freedom the Skaardrithadon promised. With all of her friends lost to the Vampire Lords what was the point? Where would she go? What would she do in the vampire-ruled Fairy Kingdom? She would become a slave eventually, wouldn't she?

138

'Pull me up. Release me.'

According to the Skaardrithadon that's the way it would be. But she didn't trust him, and while she had a breath to breathe she would do everything in her power to stop the vampires. Despite the odds, she would fight them with all her might. But not today. Today was a time of retreat.

'Pull me up.'

And there were new things to learn and discover. What or who was this new force inside her, giving her immense strength and confidence? What had happened to Zarlan-Jagr? And then there was the vampire DNA issue. Would she give up hope of one day reversing the effect of the vampire blood infecting all of her friends? Maybe – out there somewhere – an antidote existed, perhaps in an ancient text, or in some wizard's head full of spells. She could return to this vault and free her friends. So many unanswered questions.

'Pull me up.'

She knew what she had to do. She pulled the Vampire Lord up but did not release him. Instead she frog-marched him through the crowds, her free hand raised, issuing warning sparks, glowing red. The vampires backed away, parted at the Skaardrithadon's request. The merging of their hands was strengthening, not diminishing. He was whimpering in agony. She had gone half way with the Vampire Lord. She'd pulled him up from the abyss, but they were joined now. She wouldn't let him free. She did not trust him. If she released him, he would kill her.

She walked with great confident strides along the narrow path, through the entrance, and out onto the ledge. She did not look back, not once.

She did not let up her pace.

'What are you doing?' the Skaardrithadon said, fear coating his voice.

Jesse Jameson ignored him. She was saying all of her goodbyes in her head, not looking back. To see them perhaps for the last time, her friends who had been changed into dark hissing strangers would have been too much. With tears in her eyes, Jesse Jameson walked over the edge with the Vampire Lord attached to her hand like a Siamese twin. She had a hostage now – the evil leader of all the Vampires. That had to count for something.

The Skaardrithadon let out a hideous cry of terror the moment they stepped over the edge. The jagged mountain peaks rose out of the twilight like enormous stakes. His legs flailed the rushing air hopelessly.

'You are taking us both to our deaths!' he bawled. 'Are you crazy?'

'Yes,' she said. 'I believe I am.'

Jesse Jameson

and the Vampire Vault

Glossary

Antelope's horn – the male Eland is the world's largest antelope and its horns are tightly twisted resembling corkscrews.

A.W.O.L. – Absent With Out Leave is a military saying which means to leave without permission.

Doers – half vampire residents of the Naargapire, who partly are controlled by the Vampire Lord.

Geeky – the word *geek* is linked with student and computer slang; one probably thinks first of a *computer geek*. However, it is one of the words American English borrowed from the vocabulary of the circus. Large numbers of travelling circuses left a cultural legacy in various and sometimes unexpected ways. For example, Superman and other comic book superheroes owe much of their look to circus acrobats, who were similarly costumed in capes and tights. The circus sideshow is the source of the word *geek,* "a performer who engaged in bizarre acts, such as biting the head off a live chicken."

Medusa – mythical Ancient Greek creature which has snake hair.

Naargapire – the vampire homeland, a kind of fairy kingdom version of the human world's Transylvania.

Platoon – a subdivision of a company of troops consisting of two or more squads or sections and usually commanded by a lieutenant.

THE JOURNEY NEVER ENDS ...

Out-Tro

So far, it seems that the Jesse Jameson series has, just like the shape-shifter herself, been through many changes, many transformations. Originally I'd envisaged just 3 JJ books – a trilogy. But after a conversation with my father-in-law, Keith, back in late 2002, the seed of 26 books came into being. It was a crazy idea – but then I like mad ideas. As the saying goes – it really did seem like a good idea at the time.

By the time book 4 was about to go to the printing press (September 2004), I was having doubts about a 26 book series. It wasn't because I didn't think I could write that many. I was confident I could. No, it was more about my sanity as a writer. I had to this date been putting out two JJ book per year. My departure away from JJ came in the form of *The Twisted Root of Jaarfindor*. It was a breath of fresh air writing *Jaarfindor*. The thought of writing two books a year for thirteen years to fulfil the quota of 26 was daunting. Creatively I was not looking forward to the prospect, even after my initial enthusiasm. I had other books to write, one-off projects, trilogies, short story collections, editing collections of new and award-winning authors (see *The New Wave of Speculative Fiction* and *When Graveyards Yawn* due to be published autumn 2005) and whatever else inspired me. Not 26 books, taking up 13 consecutive years! So the new JJ books will probably be published at a one a year rate for the next three years. *The Stonehenge of Spelfindial* (Oct 2005), *The Earthwitch of Evenstorm* (Oct 2006), and the final book (yes, the final book 7)

The Walkers of the Worlds (Oct 2007). That allows me to write other books apart from JJ stuff.

For those of you who regularly visit my website, you'll have read that I began the JJGG in the autumn of 2001. Sitting here almost three years on, it seems that JJ has been a welcome, but long-staying lodger. And by now you'll have read Book 4 and may be as surprised as I was at the outcome of events. The possibilities for Book 5 are endless. I'll say no more just in case you've done what I do a lot, just jump around looking for clues. I'll give none here.

So, with regret and a bit of relief, I guess, if I'm honest, JJ has to leave me a lot sooner than I'd originally considered. Come October 2007, JJ will say her final goodbye. Of course, *The Twisted Root of Jaarfindor* is set in the same dimensions as the JJ books, going back in time to Elriad, the home of the Union of Thirteen. I don't think I could ever completely turn my back on the places I've created, even though some of the characters might not feature in my books again.

I hope this clears up any rumours out there about the future of the Jesse Jameson series. To everyone who's bought my books, as a collector's item or simply as an entertaining read – a big thanks.

Sean Wright
August 2004

sean wright

Jesse Jameson

and the Golden Glow

This is where it all begins. Jesse discovers that behind her seemingly normal everyday life, there is a dark hidden world. Few know about it, let alone enter in search of a mother abducted by the evil that lives there...

Book 1

in the highly acclaimed

Alpha to Omega Series

'Highly recommended.'

GP Taylor, bestselling children's author.

www.crowswingbooks.co.uk

seɑn wRIGhꞇ

Jesse Jameson

and the Bogie Beast

Jesse has little choice but to return to the
dark hidden worlds in search of her father
and her best friend. Can she overcome the
dark forces hell-bent on stopping her?

Book 2

in the highly acclaimed

Alpha to Omega Series

'Wright's world is hard to get out of my head.'
cool-reads.co.uk

www.crowswingbooks.co.uk

SEAN WRIGHT

Jesse Jameson

and the Curse of Caldazar

Immersed in a world of dark magic and frightening monsters, Jesse embarks on an impossible quest. If she can unleash the Curse of Caldazar she will save millions from the evil of the Vampire Lord...

Book 3

in the highly acclaimed

Alpha to Omega Series

'The latest star in a golden age of fantasy books for children.' *Eastern Daily Press*

<u>www.crowswingbooks.co.uk</u>

sean WRIGhT

Jesse Jameson

and the Stonehenge of Spelfindial

Jesse Jameson's adventures continue in this – the fifth - book in the series. What demons and darkness will Jesse find herself up against this time? How will she use her growing powers of transformation?

Book 5

in the highly acclaimed

Alpha to Omega Series

'Fast becoming a classic series.'
Alison Cresswell, producer of JK Rowling's Omnibus documentary.

www.crowswingbooks.co.uk